OVERLOOKING
THE
OBVIOUS

OVERLOOKING
THE
OBVIOUS

James R. Fox

ABSOLUTELY AMAZING eBOOKS

ABSOLUTELY AMAZING eBOOKS

Published by Whiz Bang LLC, 926 Truman Avenue, Key West, Florida 33040, USA.

For information contact:
Publisher@AbsolutelyAmazingEbooks.com

ISBN-13: 978-1945772887
(Absolutely Amazing Ebooks)
ISBN-10: 1945772883

For Jackie my daughter's Tara, Erin Terri, my grandsons Kyle, Daniel, Benjamin, my brother Thom and my sister Marilyn. To Mike and Joe for my family and friends, all the best, and God bless.

Romans 1:28 God gave them over to a reprobate mind.

Ephesians 5:14 Awake thou that sleepest, and arise from the dead.

Job 5:7 Yet man is born unto trouble, as the sparks fly upward.

OVERLOOKING
THE
OBVIOUS

1

The wedding announcements were sent out months ago; now the day has finally arrived. The mother of the bride is in a tizzy. Sylvia Stone is a nervous wreck. She has so much on her mind and she wants to make sure that nothing has been neglected. She huddles with her sons Sid and Teddy. Sylvia looks at her watch as she paces back and forth waiting for the father of the bride to arrive.

"So where is he?" she asked. "The most important day in our daughter's life and he is late. Just you wait and see what I give to him when he gets here." A waiter walks by carrying a tray of fluted glasses filled with champagne. Sid takes two gives one to his mother. She downs it then pulls the other glass from his hand.

The mother of the groom, Brenda Fishman, taps Sylvia on her shoulder. She is not happy with the delay of the wedding ceremony. "You know, Sylvia, our guests are beginning to wonder if you daughter is having second thoughts about becoming the new Mrs. Herb Fishman."

Sylvia grabs Brenda by her wrist. "My daughter is well prepared to be married and as soon as my husband arrives we will start the proceedings. So until then, stuff your face and drink up to your hearts content. Got that?"

Sylvia releases her wrist. "Well I never!" Brenda gasped as she quickly walks away.

Right on the dot of 7 the doors to the main entrance of the Catskills Country Club are opened. Doctor Milton Stone arrives along with Morgan Fletcher. The doctor walks with a pronounced limp attributed to polio that he contracted as a young boy. Fletcher helps the doctor with his cashmere overcoat. Sylvia has daggers in her eyes.

"Where have you been? Do you know what time it is? The klezmer band all the way from Chicago is charging us $300 an hour. What have you got to say for yourself?"

He looked right past her, eyeing up the crowd. He nods to his sons who wave back at him.

Teddy pins a pink carnation on his father's lapel. The photographer takes a couple of quick shots with his camera, and then blends into the gathering. Shelly Fishman, the groom's father, saunters over, his mouth full of crackers and cream cheese. "So at last you made it." He spit out bits of pieces on his rented tuxedo. Brenda wiped away the crumbs and gives him a nasty scowl.

"Let's get this shindig underway," the doctor replied. The master of ceremonies Billy Greene, who is gay, tapped the microphone to get everyone's attention. "Ladies and gentlemen, welcome to the renowned Catskills Country Club where such notables from Al Jolson, Jack Benny, Milton Berle, Georgie Jessel, Henny Youngman, Sophie Tucker, Frank Sinatra, Martin and Lewis have graced this very stage. Now this evening two more names will become perhaps famous. Why, because they are about to be married here tonight. So without further ado I will turn over the proceedings to the Grand Rebbe. Here he is all the way from Tel Aviv – Lieb Weintraub. Can I get a drumroll, if you would please?"

A smattering of applause is heard as the wedding begins. The four groomsmen proceed down the aisle carrying the chuppah canopy. They commence to stand at the left side of the altar. Then the groom arrives with his parents. They take their seats as their son Herb joins the groomsman. All eyes are now turned to see Mr. and Mrs. Stone's daughter Karen at the back of the grand room. Sid and Teddy escort Sylvia to her seat. She began to sob as the emotions of the ceremony get to her. "Poppa, I am so nervous. I hope I don't embarrasses you."

He holds her hand and pats her arm. "You'll do just fine. You are my little princess. You'll always be and don't you ever forget it."

She squeezed his hand. "Oh poppa, I love you so much. I only hope I can be the wife to Herb that momma has been to you all these years."

The band strikes up "Here Comes the Bride" as they walk down the aisle, up to the front of the altar. The father raises her veil ever so slightly to give his daughter a kiss. Then he lowers the veil in place. The Grand Rebbe addresses the wedding guests. "I am getting too old for this," he says as laughter filled the air. "No, seriously, the traveling back and forth, the security checks in the airports, the lousy food, the traffic, oy gavelt! Anyway this wedding is special and I'll tell you why that is. We have two great kids, am I right?" The guests clap and nod their heads in agreement.

"Right, I mean the groom's family, the Fishman's, don't they have the best kosher delicatessen in the city? And as for the Stones, well, is there a better physician than Milton? I think not." He motions for the bride and groom to join with him at the altar. They are wrapped in a prayer shawl, the talis, and drink wine. The Grand Rebbe speaks in Hebrew and English reciting passages from the Old Testament. The best man hands the Grand Rebbe a solid gold wedding band, which he blesses. He blesses the ring and tells the groom to place it on the bride's finger in a symbol of fidelity, love, and trust.

Once this is done, the best man places a wine glass wrapped in a white cloth under the bridegroom's right foot. Herb steps on the glass, which symbolizes the destruction of the temple in Jerusalem. All the guests shout, "Mazel Tov!"

"You may now kiss the bride."

Herb lifts Karen's veil and through closed eyes they enjoy a fast kiss. The band begins to play the Hora the dance where the married couple is lifted up in chairs that are carried on the shoulders of the guests. Among the many guests, is the governor, Mickey Como, an old friend of the father of the bride "Have you tried the cold cuts, Mickey?"

"No, not yet." "Here, you must try the tongue; it was just sliced. I ordered it specifically for you."

"Thanks, Milt, but I have to say I never tasted tongue. I'm partial to a good pastrami or corned beef on rye."

"Trust me, Mickey, this tongue is to die for. Here, let me make a sandwich for you."

Stone grabs two slices of Jewish rye, then takes the tongue, adds some mustard and a dill pickle on the side of the plate. The governor takes a bite. "So, what do you think?"

Como smiled back at him between the bites. "I must say it has a distinct taste unlike any other meat I've ever had. Where did you get this? Don't tell me it's from Fishman's deli."

Stone waves the back of his hand over the plate. "Fishman is a schmuck, knows nothing about the business."

"So why did you allow the marriage to take place?"

Stone gets closer to Como so others won't hear their conversation. "There's something you being a shagetz, a male gentile won't understand. When Jews get married it is never for love. It is arranged by the families, a tradition that goes back thousands of years. The Lubavich and the Satman Hasidic rarely if ever see eye to eye. That is why the Grand Rebbe officiated over the wedding. He was a survivor of Treblinka, the concentration camp of the Nazis during WWII. They killed his mother, father, and sister. Ask him to show you the tattoo on his arm. The Nazis numbered them like they were animals in a zoo."

As the night creeps along, Sid has been checking out all the single women. One of the bridesmaids, Donna Shapiro, a cute brunette, smiles at him. He walks over to her table and after a few minutes they are inside a dark closet. They start to kiss; it gets intense. Sid said to Donna, "Lift your dress and I'll do the rest."

Sid's brother Teddy is looking for him. He passes the closet in the hall and hears Donna moaning with delight. Teddy cracks a grin, downs his drink, and then returns to the ballroom. He takes a seat at the table. Sid and Donna walk in, their faces are red as beets.

"God, I love weddings."

"So true but never yours brother."

"You got that right, Teddy. If you want to get laid, you need to get your nose out of the books. Look at me, I work out, dress to impress the ladies. I have no strings to tie me down, come and go as I please."

Karen and Herb are making the rounds accepting envelopes filled with cash and checks from their guests. "Brother you need to get a life, living home with momma and poppa, jerking off in your bed, and for what?"

"I'm saving myself, Sid. Once I become a rabbi, then I'll take a wife."

"Teddy, you're going bald, you're short, plus those long curls on the side of your face, and top if off with your initials on the yarmulke. Yeah, you're one hell of a catch for any prospect."

Morgan Fletcher motions to the doctor it is time to leave. Stone gets up from his chair and whispers into Sylvia's ear. She is clearly upset. Standing next to the bar is Finn McCoole, an Irishman from Belfast, who has a thick Irish brogue. He oversees a bunch of bars in the five boroughs, plus Nassau and Suffolk Counties. He downs his drink and sits down next to Sid and Teddy.

"Well, if it isn't Mick the Prick, how the hell you doin'?" asked Sid.

"Good. The business is flowin', you guys should pay me a visit. I could hook you up with some hot tamale's I know."

"I'm good, Finn, but maybe Teddy. What do you say, brother?"

Teddy's face is beet-red, he is so embarrassed. "Don't tell me, you're a virgin? You haven't had your cherry popped yet?"

"He's going be a rabbi, Finn."

"Yeah, and I was going to be a priest until I got the calling from some hooker on the corner of my block. I never went back to church again."

The doctor and Fletcher are ready to leave. Stone tells Sid to take Sylvia and Teddy home. He kisses his sons and shakes Finn's hand. He is about to depart, then abruptly turns around. "Try the tongue, Finn. It's to die for."

"How come your old man has a black guy with him?" Finn asked Sid.

"Morgan's been working for him for years. He once was a boxer. My father took a shine to him after seeing him in the ring."

"Jews and the blacks, no wonder why everything is all screwed up in this world of ours"

"Let's not go there."

The conversation slowly peters out as the wedding guests say their goodbyes and depart. It will take a few hours to drive back to Sheepshead Bay where the Stones reside. Karen and Herb will start their new lives in the town of Kiryas Joel, near the town of Monroe in Orange County. The community was established by the Satman Hasidic sect so that families could relocate from the tiny and cramped apartments in Brooklyn. Herb's father Shelly had to grease some palms, most notably Nathan Gluckman, a greedy son of a bitch. Gluckman owns several apartment buildings in Williamsburg. He would take the gelt (money) and in return they were beholding to him in debt. Herb who was a lazy good-for-nothing who never worked a day in his life was given a job collecting the garbage in the community.

It was demeaning work and he resented his father for allowing this to happen. He would take it out on Karen. It started out first as verbal insults, but as the days turned into weeks it became physical. She would call her mother and cry, saying she wasn't happy, but Sylvia assured her it would pass and things would get better.

Unexpectedly one day, Sid popped in for a visit. Karen answered the door in her bathrobe. Her eyes were swollen and there were black and blue bruises on her arms and neck.

"What the hell happened to you, sis?"

Karen tried to avoid making eye contact with Sid. "I fell in the shower this morning."

Sid knows she's lying to him. "Where's Herb?"

"He's at work picking up the trash."

"Oh, he is, is he?" Sid gives Karen a kiss. "Put on some clothes and make a pot of coffee, this won't take long."

2

A car pulls into the parking lot near the walking trail at Peekamoose Mountain. The driver turns off the lights as the girl in the passenger seat opens her purse and applies red lipstick. "So did you bring protection, you know party hats?"

The boy checks his wallet and the pockets of his jeans. "Oh shoot, I forgot ... now what?"

The girl starts to unbutton her blouse, then – presto! – pulls out a condom from her bra. "I'm always prepared just like the Girl Scouts."

The boy is nervous, now he has to take a leak. So he tells her to wait a minute, he'll be right back. He opens the car door then walks a few paces into the woods.

"Hurry back, don't you be long" she said.

He unzips his fly to empty his bladder. He then notices a shiny object in the bushes. He zips up and walks on over to take a closer look. He can't believe his eyes. He quickly sprints back to the car, opens the door, and hops in.

The girl asks, "Are you okay?"

"Can I use your cellphone?"

"Sure, how come? Don't tell me you never had sex before."

"No, I need to call the police."

"The police? What have you done?"

"Nothing. There is a body in the woods and it looks like he was murdered."

"Murdered? No way. " She takes a look around. Their car is the only one in the parking lot. "We better drive to a safer place to make the call."

"So I guess sex is off the table for tonight?"

"Yes, but makeup sex is so much better."

The 911 operator answers in a friendly female voice: "911, what is your emergency?"

"There is a dead body in the Peekamoose Park."

"Say again please."

"I found a dead body in the park."

"Hold on while I transfer you to the local police."

In for the night, sound asleep is Holly and Jasper Fast. Jasper is the sheriff of Chirp, the closest town to the park. The phone rings on the night table and Holly nudges him to wake up.

He reaches for the phone. "Hello, this had better be important."

The 911 operator tells him about the recently received call.

"Okay, put them on."

"We want to report a dead body that's in the park." Holly rolls over, opens an eye and asks him what it's all about? Jasper waves his arm over her. "Give me a sec and I'll tell you," he said as he cups the phone with his other hand. "Are you in the park?"

"No sir, we were too scared to stay there, so I drove on over to the Dairy Queen just down the road a ways."

"Good, now just stay put. I'll be there shortly."

Jasper hangs up the phone. "Damn kids." He throws off the covers and climbs out of bed. Buck naked, he stumbles around in the dark. Buford, their bulldog, is lying beside the fireplace, snorting and snoring. Jasper picks up his boxer shorts, socks, T-shirt, uniform pants, shirt, and hat. "I have to go. Something about a body at Peekamoose. It happens all the time, right around Halloween. I won't be long, Holly." He gives her a peck on the forehead.

"Take Buford along, he needs to be walked."

Jasper taps the dog with the tip of his boot. Buford rolls over to be petted.

The black-and-white patrol car pulls up next to the pea-green Saturn at the Dairy Queen. It is the only car in the lot. Jasper rolls down his window. He recognizes the two teenagers. He checks his watch. It is a few minutes after 1 a.m.

"Kind of late to be out this time of night, Jeff Crawford and Tammy Taft," he said.

"We snuck out, sheriff, please don't tell our parents," Tammy pleads with him.

Buford pops his head up in the back seat; he is panting and clawing on the collar of Jasper's jacket. He tells Jeff to drive back to the park and he'll follow him. They arrive at the parking lot and Jasper gets out with Buford. Jeff points to the spot where he discovered the body.

"Okay, you and Tammy stay in the car while I investigate the scene."

"Yes sir, sheriff, thank you," Jeff replied.

Jasper turns on his flashlight as he nears the walking trail, Buford by his side. The flashlight illuminates the bushes, twigs, brambles, and the body of a man. Jasper crouches down to take a closer look. The hands are behind the back cinched with black zip ties; also the legs. The body is lying face down.

Jasper pulls on a pair of latex gloves, then gently rolls it over. He notices a metal wire wrapped tightly around the throat. He checks the pockets of the pants shirt and jacket for a possible ID. He comes up empty. The body is in full rigor. It appears it hasn't been disturbed by anyone or the wild animals. Buford takes off after a squirrel and disappears out of sight.

On the face of the body is dried blood around the mouth and chin. Jasper picks up a twig and shoves it into the mouth, then pries it open. The mouth is missing a tongue. Jasper has a flashback to when he was serving duty as a jarhead Marine in the Middle East. ISIS would torture their captives for hours on end, then rip out their tongues and eyes and behead them. Other times the victims were torched to death.

Buford scampers back from doing his duty in the woods. Whoever committed this crime it was personal, a way of getting even to send a message of intent. Jasper removes the gloves, then walks back to the teenagers in their car.

"You did the right thing, Jeff and Tammy, by calling in what you saw. It's getting late so motor on home."

Jeff starts up the Saturn. Jasper leans in real close to Jeff's face. "Whatever you do, don't tell a soul about this. Keep a real tight lid on it, savvy?"

"Sure thing, sheriff, cross our hearts," Tammy replied.

"Good, now you be careful going home. I'll be in touch should I need additional information."

He watches the car drive away, then places a call to County General Hospital. "This is Sheriff Fast from Chirp. I'm at Peekamoose Park by the hiking trail in the visitor's parking lot. I need an ambulance to transport a John Doe forthwith." Jasper jots down in his little black book the details fresh in his mind for further reference.

Prior to the medical examiner performing the autopsy, the sheriff will have taken samples of the fingerprints to send off to CODIS in case the John Doe is already in the justice system and has prior convictions. As luck would have it, there is a hit. The murdered man is Nick Morosco who did a nickel (5 years) at Riker's Island Prison. His last known address was in Gravesend Brooklyn. Sheriff Fast notifies the 61st Police Precinct close to the residence of Morosco.

Detective Bruce Pickett answers the call. He is an Army veteran who served two tours in Afghanistan and has PTSD. He is single and has a steady girlfriend. He alerts his partner, Chuck Dobbs, tapping him on the shoulder to get his attention. Dobbs is married with two children; he is a big Rangers fan.

Pickett takes down the information from the sheriff and then ends the call. "That was a Sheriff Jasper Fast up in the sticks. Does the name Nick Morosco ring a bell?"

Dobbs chews on his pencil. "Hm, Morosco ... how old is he?"

"Was, Chuck. Now he is dead. Age 42, was part of a B&E (breaking and entering) crew, small stuff. They dealt in smash and grab, then fenced the loot in the local's bars to make a fast buck."

The detectives knock on the captain's door. Captain Glen Millwood has more than 30 years on the job, has lost his younger brother Harry, who was killed on 9/11 when the Twin Towers came down. He still hasn't got over it and is seeing a shrink (a psychiatrist) to deal with his emotions.

"Enter. What's on your mind?"

The detectives relate to their boss all that they know about Morosco.

"Check his jacket in the file cabinet, some of the old cases aren't updated into the computer database."

"Will do, Cap," replied Pickett.

They find the case file on Morosco. The last one to see him was his PO (parole officer) who flipped him into a CI (Confidential Informer). Last time they made contact was two months ago.

Pickett and Dobbs leave the precinct, then get into an unmarked car and proceed to drive away. While they are cruising down Kings Highway they pass bodegas, pizza joints, Chinese takeout stores. One after the other, the signs are posted in foreign languages.

"Did you hear about Tucker getting reassigned to the mayor's detail?"

"He's a douchebag."

"Who Tucker?"

"No, Chuck, the ass wipe who thinks he runs the city. He hates us, has no regard for the cops. He sides with Sharpton and his cronies."

"Did you hear about Crapaknack paying a visit to the cons at Riker's the other day? He can't get a job as QB in the NFL"

"Serves him right takin' a knee for Black Lives Matter. Bullshit to that. We got blacks among the ranks who risk their lives day in day out, plus all those in the military keeping us safe."

"What about Trump, and all the big wigs, being accused of sexual misconduct."

"Give me a break, Bruce. Who hasn't made a pass at a hot chick? This political correctness or whatever you want to call it is a joke. I mean JFK had Marilyn Monroe in his bed when Jackie wasn't there. They all do it, but now the women are making it a big deal just to take the men down."

"Same with the Church. The Pope turns his eyes away from what's going on."

"Politics and religion are like oil and vinegar."

"Absolutely, Bruce," Chuck said.

They pull up to an apartment building where Morosco lived. The front door has a piece of cardboard covering a hole for the broken piece of glass. The doorbells to the apartment read like a who's who: Patel, Singh, Chou Ortega Gold, but none for Morosco. Dobbs rings the bells at random to gain access into the building. The inside door buzzes and they enter.

"So where do want to start up or down?"

"I'll do the top floors, Bruce. I could use the exercise."

Most of the tenants are afraid to answer their door. fearful of ICE who will take them into custody for being in the country without proper documentation. Gold in apartment 4C opens her door. She is in her late 80's and lets them in.

"Mrs. Gold, we are detectives. Can you tell us what apartment Mr. Morosco lives in?"

"Mr. Morosco, he's in 5D. Keeps to himself, but I haven't seen him in quite some time. Is he alright?"

"No, we have a bit of bad news. Someone did him harm and now he's dead."

She clutches her chest and needs help getting to the sofa in the living room. "That's terrible how ... where ... when did this happen? Please don't tell me it was here in the building."

"No, Mrs. Gold, it was far from here. Do you know where we can find the super? We need to get into Morosco's apartment to look for anything that could provide us a lead to whom could have done him any harm."

"The super – oy gavult, he's useless that drunk. Take a look at my bathroom ceiling, it leaks whenever the people upstairs take a shower. It's a good thing I'm on rent control. Do you know what the rents are going for these days? Highway robbery. I'm an old lady, but they treat me like dirt. You know something, I'm the only one who speaks English in the building."

The detectives have heard enough and leave her their card with the phone number to call if she needs them. They start to walk back to the car when Dobbs spots a bar across the street. They enter the Two

Timer's. It is early in the afternoon so there are but a few customers and the bartender. The owner of the bar is Tyrone Trigger O'Neil. Born in County Roscommon, he worked his way up through the ranks of the Mafia. Lucky Luciano and Frank Costello hated the Irish but not for O'Neil. In 1957 at the Park Sheraton Hotel, Albert Anastasia was seated in a barber chair. His bodyguard took a walk and two hit men fired 10 shots fatally killing Anastasia. Even though there were 11 eyewitnesses the cops could not arrest the killers. One of the killers was O'Neil and Joey Gallo bragged that he was part of the rub out. O'Neil was presented a .45 Colt nickel-plated and pearl-handle gun from the Mafia that is mounted in his office in the back of the bar.

The Two Timer's is dimly lit, the smell of pine sawdust and lingering tobacco and onions fill the air. The beer taps drip; a large jar of pickled eggs is displayed on the old worn dark oak bar. There is a black and white photograph of the 1955 World Champion Brooklyn Dodgers signed by the team that hangs on the wall. There is a nude photo of a woman that is believed to be of Amelia Earhart. There is also a set of boxing gloves signed by Sugar Ray Robinson and a horseshoe for good luck. Above the bar in large brass letters the motto of Tyrone Trigger O'Neil: BEHAVE OR BE GONE. And where would a good Irish bar be without a sign that states SLAINTE, good health? That sign hangs above the office.

"What'll it be?" Connor O'Roarke asks the detectives in his thick Irish brogue as he wipes down the bar with a bar mop.

"NYPD. We're looking for a Nick Morosco; he lives across the street" Pickett said.

"Nope, I never heard the name. Sorry."

Dobbs pulls out a photo of Morosco taken after he was killed, slides it across the bar to O'Roarke. "Like I said, never heard the name and lookin' at the face it don't ring a bell."

Dobbs snatches the photo, then goes through the bar asking the customers if they know him.

A woman in the back booth, smoking a cigarette and sipping a glass of beer, nods her head. "Nick 'The Quick' Morosco. Yeah, I know him. What has he done now?"

The detectives slide into the booth across from her. "He's dead. Do you know anybody that would do him any harm?" Pickett asked her.

She takes a drag and taps the glass with her cubic zirconia ring. "Take a number, detectives. Nick was a nice guy, don't get me wrong, but he was running with the wrong crowd. "

"You got a name for us to connect Nick with, so we can solve his murder?" Dobbs asked her.

The bartender is giving her the evil eye, then males a gesture with his finger of a knife slitting her throat. She gets the message all right. She puts out the cigarette; her composure has quickly changed. "I just remembered I got to pick up my niece at the bus stop." She slides out of the booth and pushes her shopping cart with a broken wheel out the front door.

The detectives move back to the bar. Dobbs asked O'Roarke, "If we were to ask you what's her name ... let me guess you wouldn't know that either"

The bartender wipes down the booth and grabs the ashtray and the empty glass.

Pickett asked him, "You just work the day shift or until closing time?"

"I do the day and there's a guy on until 3 a.m. "

"We didn't get you name," said Pickett.

"The name's Connor O'Roarke."

" Who's on at night?"

"That would be Buster Coogan, but I doubt if he would know who you're looking for."

"Tell him we might pay him a visit," said Dobbs.

As the detectives walked out of the bar, Pickett commented to Dobbs, "Ireland the Emerald Isle – a plethora of poets, politicians, pugilists, and procrastinators."

To which Dobbs replied, "Of which there are cops, firefighters, lawyers, priests, and nuns. It is truly a smorgasbord that would drive any saint or sinner to drink himself into a stupor."

No sooner do they leave when O'Roarke makes a phone call. "Finn it's me Connor. A pair of detectives just left the bar askin' about Nick Morosco. No, I didn't tell the anything. But one of the regulars, Mary Dunham, flapped her gums. Opened her pie hole wide as can be, sayin' she knows him. Okay, Finn, you'll take care of it."

3

At the Stone's home dinner was always on the table at the dot of 6. Sid had a standing reservation to attend ever since he moved out and found a place of his own. Tonight they were dining on brisket. Milt sat at the head of the table with Teddy on his left and Sylvia on the end. The front door opened and Sid entered. He takes off his coat and hangs it in the hall closet, then seats himself next to Milt.

"So how was your day?" asked Sylvia as she passed the platter of meat.

"Good, Ma, thanks. I've been keeping busy at work. The real estate business has been slow, but now that Trump is the president prices have skyrocketed."

"Trump, what a joke. He Twitters away like a meschugena about every little thing."

Teddy passed the bowl of red cabbage to Milt. "Donald has moxie. He named Jerusalem the capital of Israel. Did any other president do that? The answer is no."

"You're so right, poppa. He'll always be on our side." Teddy took a bite of the brisket.

"Rabbi Block commented on it today at the yeshiva."

Sylvia throws up her hands in frustration. "Enough of this; talking about Trump already. Oh how I miss Karen being with us."

Sid took a sip of the Manishewitz wine. "I knew there was something to tell you, ma. I paid her a visit the other day."

Sylvia looked surprised as she nibbled on the Brussel sprouts. "Hm I wonder why she never mentioned it when she called this morning?"

After dinner while Sylvia was clearing the table, Sid whispered into his father's ear. "Karen's husband has been mistreating her."

Milt clenched his fist. "But I set him straight; I made him an offer or else."

The father kissed his eldest son. "Teddy, join us in the den. There is something I want to tell you."

Sylvia placed the dirty dishes, glassware, and utensils into the dishwasher. "Well, I'm off to Rochelle's to play Mahjong. I'll be back before 11. Sid, you be careful driving home. Teddy, you be in bed no later than 10." She grabbed her purse and coat, then out the door she went.

The doctor lit up a Macanudo cigar and poured himself a snifter of brandy. "Sid, first thing tomorrow morning set up a meeting with Finn McCoole. Make a reservation at Lundy's for lunch. Teddy, here is where you come in. I have a job for you."

"But, poppa, what about my schooling? I have so little time to do anything but study."

Sid shook his head. "Teddy, forget about being a rabbi. Step up and grow a set of balls."

"Sid, don't talk to your brother like that. We don't live in the ghetto."

"Sorry, pop, I'm just trying to help him out."

Milt tapped the cigar into the ashtray. "There has been a change of personnel, so now I need a replacement and, Teddy, this is where you come in."

"Poppa, you want me to help you out at the office?" Sid shot a glance at his father.

"No, not at my office. You'll be working with Mr. McCoole."

"Pop, he can't work with him, you can't be serious."

"Sid, I know what I'm doing. Just make the call to him and when we're at Lundy's I'll lay out all of my plans. Now let me be alone so that I can unwind."

A few moments passed, his glass is empty and the cigar had been smoked down to the stub. Stone made a call to Fletcher. "Bring the car around."

Stone grabbed a handful of pill bottles, tucked them into a black medical bag, then entered Teddy's bedroom where he was reading the Torah. "I have to step out to see one of my patients. Tell momma I'll be back as soon as I can."

Seated in the backseat of his car, Fletcher asked him, "Where to?"

"Take me uptown to 147th and Lex."

Fletcher smiled back at him in the rearview mirror and asked, "Are you going to see the black sugar queen tonight? She is fine, mighty fine indeed, hot damn Uncle Sam!"

They proceed along Surf Avenue, then to the Belt Parkway onto the BQE and over the RFK Bridge. "I hate that they have changed the name of the Triboro to the RFK, just like renaming the Queensborough to the Ed Koch Bridge."

"I agree with you, doctor, although the Jackie Robinson Parkway sounds better than the Interboro."

Fletcher looked back at Stone. "You're pretty quiet. Is there something on your mind?"

"It is my daughter Karen. Her good-for-nothing husband Herb has been giving her a hard time. I knew there was a reason why I didn't like that son-of-a-bitch."

"Is there anything I can do? Just say the word and it's done."

"Thanks, I know I'll give it time to see how it goes."

"You know, Doctor Stone, if it wasn't for you, I don't know where I'd be today. You found me when I wasn't that fast anymore in the ring. I started taking dope and getting into trouble."

"Believe it or not, I saw in you my reflection of what I wanted to be, playing sports, but I contracted polio and that ended any chance of being an athlete."

"Just think if our lives were reversed and you were driving me and I was sitting in the backseat."

The doctor looked out the window and smiled at the words just spoken. How lucky he is to have been born white, a Jew who had the ability to make something of himself, and the luck of the draw that nobody has before they are born. All men are not created equal. In order to get himself free of his doldrums Doctor Stone told Fletcher to play some music.

"How about 'I Want To Be Sedated' by the Ramones or 'We Didn't Start the Fire' by Billy Joel?"

"No, I'm not in the mood for rock and roll; how about some jazz or classical. You make the choice."

"I have just what the doctor ordered. So sit back and relax."

Luciano Pavarotti's voice is heard through the car speakers as they travel through the streets of Harlem. At last they reach their destination. Fletcher pulls up in front of a fancy brownstone, waiting while Stone climbs out of the backseat. "Give me a half-hour, no more no less."

"Yes sir, Doctor Stone, you take care and tell Miss Sweet Magnolia I said hi."

Stone used the wrought iron railing to assist him up the steep brownstone steps to the frosted glass front doors. He rang the doorbell to be let in. A brown-skinned woman wrapped in a multicolored kimono greets him at the door. She is strikingly beautiful, tall with hazel eyes, high cheekbones. Her hair is closely cropped, her teeth white as ivory. She is obviously happy to see Stone as she gives him a long and tender kiss on the lips.

"How was your trip from Brooklyn? I hope the traffic wasn't too bad."

Stone unbuttons the overcoat and tossed it on the overstuffed chair next to the door. "Fletcher said hi."

She smiles at him. "Oh, he's so sweet, always calls me Miss Sweet Magnolia because of where I'm from. You know, Milt, we grew up not far from one another, both of us poor as the day is long. And now look at me living the high life in Harlem. Yes siree, this tar baby girl has made a name for herself, from being Belinda Bellows to Miss Sweet Magnolia, the highest-paid hooker in all of New York."

Stone and she get down to business, undressing each other, and then into the king-size bed. She gave him what he came for and he in return provided the pills. Uppers, downers, bennies – just what she needed to help her get through until they meet again.

4

Ever since getting a whopping from his brother-in-law, Herb Fishman is out for revenge. He resented having to work for a living, hated that his father would not come to his aid and give him a share of the deli business. Add to that is that Karen is not the wife he expected her to be.

The last few weeks Karen had been having morning sickness so she called her mother for advice. Sylvia is ecstatic with the news. "Mazel tov, my little bubala is pregnant. Oh, my prayers have been answered!"

"Momma, I haven't been tested yet to see if I am."

"So what are you waiting for? Go to the drugstore and pick up a test kit."

"Momma, there are strict rules in Kiryas Joel. You can only go to the Hasidic doctors. Momma, I want poppa to examine me. Is he home?"

"No, Karen, but as soon as he is home I'll have him call you. So how is Herb? I was told that Sid paid you a visit. Was your husband happy to see him?"

Karen started to cry. "Momma, I have to go now. Herb just got home from work and it takes a while for him to unwind."

Herb slams the door closed. "Who were you talking to on the phone?"

Karen wiped her nose and eyes. "My mother. Did you have a good day at work?"

"Do I look like I did? Do I smell like I just came out of the shower and put on cologne and deodorant? Hell no, I stink from head-to-toe picking up all the rotten vegetables, fish, and God only knows what else."

Herb removed the sunglasses that hid the black eyes he had received from Sid. "Is dinner ready or have you forgotten to make it?"

"It'll be done soon. Go take a shower and by the time you're done I'll have it on the table."

No sooner have they sat down to eat, Herb took a bite of the gefilte fish then spit it out. Then he tossed the plate against the wall.

"You can't do anything right! You are useless to me. I wish you were dead."

She doesn't know what to say or do. Karen was going to tell him that she might be pregnant but now is not the time. Karen ran into the bedroom, then closed and locked the door.

"Are you locking me out of my bedroom? Open the damn door!"

He jiggled the doorknob, then he kicked it. Finally he used his shoulder to force it open. Karen is filled with terror for her life. Herb is in a rage. He smacks her in the face. She falls into the bed. Herb grabbed her hairbrush from the dressing table. He straddled her and continued to beat her until the rage inside of him was spent. Karen's face was a bloody mess; it is then that Herb realized what he had done.

"Go ahead, call your brother. I'll give him a reason to pay us another visit. Only this time he'll look a lot worse than you."

Karen coughed up blood as she tried to breathe. Herb doesn't know what to do. He must call for help, but what should he say had happened to his wife? He grabbed the phone, then hesitated. He had to make it sound as if he found her this way. He places the call.

Then while waiting for the EMS to arrive, he dashes around the apartment, cleaning up the mess in the kitchen to cover his tracks.

The ambulance arrived, two burly men wearing yarmulkes of blue and white the colors of the Israeli flag proudly displayed on their heads. They pushed a stretcher and carried medical tote bags into the apartment. Herb directed them into the bedroom.

"How did this happen?"

"I don't know I just came home from work and found her this way. My God, will she be alright?" He sat down at the kitchen table.

"It doesn't look good."

The team hooked her up to a transportable device that monitors her vital signs that is relayed to the hospital. They took her blood pressure and wiped her face clean of the blood.

"Do you think she was molested ... or raped?"

"We have no idea. Only a doctor will be able to determine that."

The paramedics gently lifted Karen from the bed onto the stretcher. They placed an oxygen mask over her nose and mouth to help her breathe. Herb sat by her side in the ambulance. They arrive at the emergency entrance of Temple Hospital where a team of nurses and interns were waiting. Herb held her hand as if he were a caring and concerned husband to the wife he loved.

Karen is moved into the ICU while Herb was escorted into the visitor's lounge. The nurse's station is a hub of activity, answering the phones, taking down information in the patient's charts, and administering to those most critical in their rooms. A bespectacled dwarf with a white goatee dressed in a white lab coat approached Herb.

"I am Doctor Simon. I will be the attending physician for your wife."

Herb was sweating profusely. The doctor noticed the blood on his shirt and that his hands were bruised. "Do you have any idea how this could have happened?"

"No, doctor, I just came home from work and found her this way. I tried to help the best that I could that is why my clothes are full of blood."

"I see it would be prudent for you to call her family they need to know as soon as possible."

The doctor started to walk away then Herb asked, "Will the police be notified?"

The doctor turned around to face him. "Here at Kiryas Joel we are self-sufficient our investigators will conduct a thorough going-over of the scene. What happens in our community stays in our community. Now, I must attend to not only your wife but to my other patient's."

Herb is terrified of Sid and the last thing he wants to see is the Stone family. So if he calls his mother Brenda to break the news and she will in turn notify the in-laws.

Shelly and Brenda arrive and shortly thereafter the family Stone. Sid has to be restrained from getting at Herb.

"What happened to Karen, you son-of-a-bitch? Did you touch her again?" Sid demanded to know.

"Again?" Brenda remarked to the accusation.

"Your son has been abusing our daughter," Milt told her.

"And you beat me up," Herb countered, pointing at Sid. "He gave me a pair of black eyes!"

"Serves you right for hitting our sister," Teddy chimed in.

Into the family feud steps Dr. Simon with the head of security for Kiryas Joel. Ziva Habbib is ex-Mossad, trim and shapely, strikingly beautiful with long black hair and big brown eyes. She has a tiny mole on her right cheek in the shape of a crescent moon. "I see that everyone is here for Karen Fishman. She is very lucky to be alive. For the time being she is on a respirator. It will be touch-and-go because she has suffered a brain hemorrhage."

"Oh my God, how did this happen? I was expecting to find out if she was pregnant. Nobody told us about her condition when Brenda called us." Sylvia glared at Brenda. "Did you know about this?"

"No, I had no idea … I am in shock. Who could have done this?"

Dr. Stone introduces Ziva, who speaks with a distinct Jewish accent. "I will be investigating what happened to Mrs. Fishman. She sustained a horrific assault. It is amazing that she survived. She is unconscious so I cannot interview her at this time. Dr. Stone has notified me that she may have some short-term memory loss."

"Dr. Simon, I am a physician. I would like to move our daughter to a hospital in Brooklyn where I can attend to her with TLC."

"I understand your concern, but I assure you we have the finest medical team money can buy," Ziva continued. "I will be viewing the surveillance cameras here at Kiryas Joel. If there is a suspect acting suspicious at the time of the assault we will bring him in for questioning."

5

Captain Glen Millwood at the 61st Precinct addressed his team of detectives. "The PC police commissioner Danny Como at 1PP (One Police Plaza) has issued a BOLO for an international terrorist. Ari Habbib is an Israeli who has been radicalized by ISIS. He is cunning, very difficult to capture. He assumes many disguises and aliases. Now that we are approaching the holidays we need to be aware of any chatter over the Internet. We are in conjunction with Interpol, the FBI, and the CIA. It is all hands on deck. I am not telling you to put your cases aside, but add this to your workload. Go about your day and let's be safe out there. The NYPD is the best at what we do. You are dismissed."

Pickett and Dobbs are seated at their desks. Dobbs has a framed photo of his wife Connie, who has blue eyes and blonde hair along with a deep dark tan. His son Bobby, age 7, has a crew cut. The kid is wearing sunglasses and a yellow tank top. Daughter Mindy, age 13, is wearing a polka-dot bikini, her hair in cornrows. The photo was taken at Ocean City, New Jersey, on the Boardwalk. Dobbs and his wife have been married going on 15 years. Pickett has a Mets baseball in a plastic cube on his desk.

"So how was the weekend?" Pickett asked Dobbs.

"Good. We took the kids ice-skating. Before you know it, they'll be lighting up the tree at Rockefeller Center. How about you? How was your weekend?"

"The usual, stayed close to home." He gave Dobbs a sly wink. "If you know what I mean."

"If only I did what you did, partner. Say, can you score me some tickets to see the Rangers? I'd like to take the kids to see a game."

"Yeah, let me give my connection a call and see what's available. Does it matter when?"

"Nope, I'll give the Captain a heads up so maybe we can move my tour around."

"Lots of luck with that. Now that we have a terrorist at large you might have a tough sell trying to get a day off."

Pickett thumbs through the stack of papers on his desk. "What are you looking for?"

"That sheriff's phone number upstate. You know, in regards to the Morosco case."

"Hold on, I have it in my cell phone. I added it just in case. Yup, here it is. Do you want me to call him?"

"Yeah, do that."

Sheriff Jasper Fast is in his office diligently at work crafting fly-fishing lures when the phone rings. "Sheriff's office – how can I help you?"

"Hi Sheriff, this is detective Dobbs of the 61st Precinct in Brooklyn. Me and my partner Pickett was wondering if you ever found any clues in regards to Nick Morosco."

"Morosco ... Morosco? Oh yeah, the fella found in the park. I have his clothes. The medical examiner determined he was strangled to death. My assumption, it was a piano wire pulled right snug up against the wind pipe."

"A piano wire, huh? Sounds like it was personal. Somebody wanted him to suffer a slow and agonizing death."

"For sure, detective. Plus there were traces of narcotics in his system. Opioids, but not enough for an overdose."

Pickett jots down notes to add to the file on Morosco. "Say, Sheriff, just where exactly are you located? I thought I knew upstate pretty good, but never heard of Chirp."

The sheriff lets out a chuckle. "Heck, most folks only find us when they get lost after exiting the Interstate. We're in the Catskills. Peekamoose Mountain is the big attraction because it has a nice place to swim at the Blue Hole. If you're ever up this way, do drop in."

"I just might take you up on your offer, Sheriff. Before you know it, my kids will be up and out of the house. I remember my dad would take us camping in the woods; it was a lot of fun. Well, you take care now."

"You too, detective. Have a great day."

Soon after the sheriff continues working on the fly-fishing lures, the front door opened. In strides a tribal elder of the Oneida Nation. That Malachi Eaglefeather is an imposing figure is an understatement. Standing a shade under 7 foot tall, he has broad shoulders, long black hair, and deep brown eyes. He is wearing a large silver belt buckle, a Navajo turquoise ring, and a similar bracelet. He is dressed in a red flannel shirt, blue jeans, and fancy red cowboy boots.

The file on Nick Morosco is lying open in plain sight on the sheriff's desk. "Well, look here, its Malachi. What brings you into town?"

"Jasper, how are you? I had to pick up some groceries and fill up the pickup truck. So while I was paying the bill I noticed the newspaper rack next to the door. The local paper has the headline stating Murder in the Park Still a Mystery."

"Yup, there isn't much to go on, Malachi. Wish I had a clue to use."

Malachi looks down at the file on the desk that has a photo of the body. "Do you mind if I take a closer look?" The sheriff hands him the photo. "I think I saw him, but he wasn't alone. He was in the backseat of a high-end Mercedes Benz. "

"When was that, Malachi?"

"Well, let me think ... it was a few days before Halloween. It was about 6 p.m. My house is the closest to the town road out by Possum Creek. I could tell right away the driver was lost because the motor was idling and the GPS gave him the wrong directions. So being nosy and cautious, I strapped on my holster and firearm, then walked up to the car. The driver's window rolled down and behind the wheel was this black bald dude and in the backseat was this guy in the photo. He was skinny and short, had a scraggly beard, dirty long hair just like in this photo."

"So it was just the black driver and him in a fancy car?"

"No, sheriff, there was another guy in the backseat, an older man. I really didn't get a good look at him. Sorry, Jasper."

"Hey, you just gave me a tip to go on. Now I'll have to figure why would someone come all the way from Brooklyn to our neck of the woods to do a murder? It was still daylight, so they had to know that dropping a body could easily have been seen by an unsuspecting eyewitness. Did you give them directions, Malachi?"

"I did. I told them how to get back on the Interstate. Maybe they had somewhere to go later and had time to kill."

"Precisely, my Indian friend. Now I must find out exactly where and why this guy Nick Morosco was killed."

6

Sylvia refused to leave Karen's room at the hospital, so Milt, Sid, and Teddy, along with Fletcher, returned to Brooklyn. Noticeably absent is Herb, who has not visited Karen since she was admitted.

Ziva has watched all of the surveillance footage of the time when Karen was attacked. There is no corroborating evidence to determine that an outsider could have committed the crime. Therefore, the only person would be her husband, Herb Fishman. He has not returned to work, so Ziva decided to pay him a visit at the apartment. She knocked on the door, but there is no answer. She had anticipated this would happen and used the spare key that was inside Karen's purse when she was brought into the hospital. Herb forgot to take it out of the purse when the ambulance arrived.

Ziva entered the apartment. There are no signs of Herb. It appears to her that he sensed the investigation would lead to him, so he packed a bag and left. Ziva has her work cut out for her.

Dr. Simon entered Karen's room. Sylvia is fast asleep in the chair next to her daughter's bed. He touched her on the arm to awaken her.

"Oh, I am so sorry, doctor. I tried to stay awake, but I must have nodded off. Is there any news as to when my daughter can come home?"

"There is nothing to do, Mrs. Stone. Why don't you go home and get some rest. Your daughter is in good hands."

Ziva arrived at the hospital room, but waited patiently for Dr. Simon to leave. "Mrs. Stone," she said, "how are you holding up?"

"I am praying for Karen to pull through."

Ziva held her hand. "Have you seen your son-in-law? I just came from their apartment, but he was not there and he hasn't showed up for work."

Sylvia looked surprised. "How could I be so blind not to see through his veil of lies? Sid, my oldest son, had an altercation with Herb. I was in total denial, refused to believe what was going on between my daughter and that schmuck. Oh, wait until I tell my husband. If he gets his hands on him, the Fishman's will soon be seating in Shiva. Mark my words."

Ziva's cell phone rings and she excused herself to take the call as she stepped out of the room. It is a text message, an alert regarding a possible terrorist threat to the entire metropolitan area. An APB advised to be on the lookout for Ari Habbib. The text continued, Take precaution if coming into contact with this individual. Do not attempt to apprehend him alone. Call for backup ASAP.

Ziva now has to trust the authorities in the pursuit of her brother. For the time being, all that matters is to find out the location of Herb Fishman.

7

The time has come for Dr. Stone and Finn McCoole to meet at Lundy's Seafood Restaurant. Lundy's is located at Sheepshead Bay, close to Coney Island. Milt, Sid, and Teddy are seated at a table that overlooks the water. There are fishing boats and yachts tied to the docks. Seagulls swoop down and snatch morsels of discarded food, then perch high on top of the restaurant roof.

Finn McCoole arrived fashionably tardy. He sat down at the table facing Milt. "I see you brought your bodyguards, Milt. Do you want to pat me down just in case I have a piece?" Finn opened his jacket to show them he is unarmed.

"Let's get down to business," Milt told him. "From now on my son Teddy will be working with us." Teddy had no idea what his father had in mind.

Finn lets out a hearty laugh. "Oh that's rich, you have to be kidding. What kind of a job is he going to do? Why just look at him, he's chubby baby fat, hasn't even shaved, I bet. I could see him in one of O'Neil's joints dressed as a Jew boy."

Milt took a forkful of salad. "When we took Nick Morosco in, you convinced me that he was someone who could be trusted. Well, guess what, Finn. He was skimming from the till, a little here a little there. Well, that's all in the past, Finn."

McCoole gestured to get the waiter's attention and ordered a round of drinks. "A couple of cops came around to my bar the other day. It seems that Nick was murdered. Do you know anything about that?"

Milt stared out the window, thinking about his daughter lying in the hospital bed fighting for her life. "He knew what he was doing, Finn, so he had to be taken out, simple as that."

Finn can't believe what he just heard. He leaned over the table so that only they can hear the conversation. "So now we're killing one another? This is not what I agreed to. I was supposed to sell your drugs in the bars and we'd split the take. Why didn't you tell me when you found out about Nick stealing from us? I could have handled it my way."

"Your way, Finn, is not how I conduct business. Trust is paramount; that is why I have Sid working for us. And now it will be Teddy's turn."

After they had read the menus, the meals were ordered and another round of drinks served. Meanwhile Sid buttered a roll, Teddy picked at his salad, and Finn stirred his drink. Milt pulled out a pad and pen from his breast pocket. "The last time I saw Nick, we had taken a ride upstate. His body was found in a picturesque location. There is a lot of opportunity for us to make a tidy sum of money. Here's where you come in, Finn. Sid and Teddy, you're included. There is an Indian casino called the Turning Stone that's just ripe for the picking. Finn, you bet heavy at the craps table. Sid and Teddy, I want you pull in the gamblers, give them samples of our pills. Once we get a connection or two, all the chips will start to stack up."

Their meals have arrived – lobster, crab, mussels, oysters, and clams all around. "If we can pull this off, the money can't be traced because the casino is on the private property of the Oneida Reservation."

"But one question, Milt. What about Nick Morosco's murder?"

"What about it?" Milt replied between bites.

"Well, what if the cops figure it out ... you know, who killed him."

"Nobody knows who did it, nobody but us seated at this table and Fletcher."

"So where is he?" Finn asked as he looked around the restaurant.

"Don't you worry about him. He's doing what he does best – TCB, taking care of business."

They continue to eat and drink, when Sid's cell phone rings. It is Sylvia. "Where are you? I just called the house, but no one picked up the phone."

"I'm with Pop and Teddy. What's up?"

"What's up, you ask? Put your father on the phone."

"Pop, it's mom. She wants to speak with you. She sounds very upset."

Sylvia gives her husband an earful in regards to Karen's condition and that Herb has disappeared without a trace. Milt shakes his head as he listens to her. "I'll take care of it," he says.

"Tell me how are you going to take care of it?"

"I have my ways, Sylvia. Now you need to come home. There isn't anything you can do for Karen. I know we want her home, but Doctor Simon knows what has to be done."

The conversation is now over. Milt tells his sons and Finn the news about Herb. "Leave him to me, Pop. That piece of crap is mine!"

~ ~ ~

Herb arrived at his parent's home in Forest Hills, Queens. Brenda opened the front door to let him in. He is shaking like a leaf, his eyes are bloodshot, he hasn't slept since he beat up his wife. Brenda is puzzled by Herb arriving unannounced. "Is everything alright? How is Karen?"

Herb paces back and forth in the living room, pauses to take a quick peek out the window, then shuts the blinds. "I did a terrible thing," he says. "I made a mistake ... I lost my temper and took it out on Karen."

Brenda is shocked at what he did. She trembles, then sat on the sofa. "You have to go back. You can't stay here, Herb. You must turn yourself in."

This is not what he wanted to hear from her. He assumed that his parents would protect him. "Where's dad?"

"Where else would he be? He's at work. Oh, how I should have listened to him when he wanted you to have a job in the deli. But no, I said, let our son enjoy being a child. And so you grew up being spoiled and coddled by me."

Herb takes notice of Brenda's purse on the dining room table. He grabs it, takes out the wallet, removes the cash and her credit cards.

"What are you doing? Give that back to me!" She grabs his arm, but he pushes her away. Brenda and Herb wrestle for her possessions. Herb shoves Brenda up against the kitchen wall and she hits her head. Her knees buckle and she slides down the wall onto the Italian marble floor. In haste Herb dashes out the door and drives away destination unknown.

8

Ever since the first rays of sun arose over the Garden of Eden, man and woman have been torn between good and evil. Cain and Abel were brothers who were jealous of one another's affection or lack therefore from Adam. "Am I my brother's keeper?" was Cain's reply to Abel's absence and ultimate death at his hands. The Middle East became a boiling cauldron from the onset of Moses combating King Pharaoh Ramses to allow passage out of Egypt into the Promised Land. The 12 tribes were divided as Moses ascended Mount Sinai to seek council from Yahweh. Moses descended the mountain holding in his hands two stone tables which contain the Ten Commandments.

The Roman Empire was not content with only governing Europe, it had plans to expand into the Middle East. Their pagan ways did not bode well for anyone who believed in the deity. The followers of Moses were no exception. To anyone who would defy Caesar a swift penalty was administered, often death by crucifixion. As the centuries passed, one by one like a row of dominoes, they became stacked, just waiting for an opportune time to be knocked down.

There had always been rumors of a World War, but it was speculative. What one event could bring about a fragile and fractured Europe into the throes of war? But an anarchist's bullet assassinated Archduke Franz Ferdinand and thus WWI was launched. Most of

Europe and Russia were engaged in fighting, using mustard gas in trench warfare. America was neutral; that is, until a torpedo fired from a German U-boat sunk the Lusitania. Millions of lives were lost on both sides. The war did not end until November 11, 1918, when peace was declared.

Germany was penalized dearly. The country was divided and it would take a miracle to reunite the masses. A restless young man who was a private in the German army during WWI began to be noticed. He would speak out against the government and was thrown into prison. While he was incarcerated, his thoughts were written down which would later become the book *Mein Kampf.*

Adolf Hitler was released from prison, then went back to work. He outfitted his followers in brown shirts and trousers and designed a twisted cross as the official insignia of the Nazi Party. Hitler's popularity could no longer be ignored. The ruling government stepped down and by doing so gave Hitler absolute power to rule over Germany. Europe held its collective breath, but did little to halt Hitler's swift rise to seize control. Winston Churchill had been in Germany and took notice of Hitler's disdain for the Jews.

"The Jews are not Germanic. They are nothing more than rodents. They infect us with their dirty habits. The only way to eradicate a rats nest is to get rid of them, every one of them." Hitler proclaimed that the Arian Nation was the Master Race that would rule for a thousand years. Hitler surrounded himself with intellectuals – scientists, physicists, architects – who would put together the final solution. It would be the extermination of the Jews throughout Germany. Concentration camps were built to be the final destination where Jews packed in cattle cars were transported by rail to remote locations. Families were separated, the men in one section, the women and children in another.

All of the Jews were tattooed with a number on their arms that was forbidden in their faith. But Hitler and the Nazis could care less about a Supreme Being. The Nazis would follow their Fuhrer into hell by doing Satan's work. Hitler's war machine consisted of Panzer tanks, the Luftwaffe air power, and a fleet of battleships, cruisers, and submarines.

Benito Mussolini, the Italian fascist, and Tojo of Japan formed an alliance with Hitler that became the Axis of Power. All of Europe with the exemption of Great Britain was in the hands of the Nazis. If the Axis could keep America neutralized, then the world would be theirs. But Tojo set his sights on taking over the Pacific, a possibility if Japan could hit the US Navy at Hawaii.

Early in the morning on December 7, 1941, squadrons of Jap Zeros dropped bombs on Battleship Row, sinking the Utah, Oklahoma, and Arizona. But they missed the most important targets, the oil supply and the aircraft carriers. Thus, America entered the war, which was won in 1945. In the aftermath of the war atrocities of what were unimaginable acts against humanity were made public. The officers and guards in charge of the concentration camps were prosecuted at the Nuremburg Trials.

One by one, those accused stated they were only following orders and were protected under the Articles of War. The Tribunal of Judges passed down sentences of death or prison without parole. The Jews were without a home in Germany. Those who had survived the horrors of being prisoners wanted to find a new place to live.

The Golan Heights, which Britain controlled, was ceded over to France in the Franco-British Agreement in 1923. In 1944, France terminated the agreement, with the land then granted to Syria. The State of Israel was established in 1948 from territory that Britain once held. At the foothills of the Golan Heights, farmers raised crops and livestock. As new Israelis arrived in the Hula Valley, a gathering of collective farms – kibbutzes – began to take roots.

The Syrians would fire their weapons randomly from the Heights, taking pot shots at the Jews and the livestock. In charge of the Syrian forces was Yasser Arafat. Israel sent a delegation to the UN in 1966 and demanded a halt to the attacks by the Fatah, the Syrian army. Syria was defiant and the Soviet Union sided with the Arabs. Israel had no other option but to retaliate.

In 1967, the Six Day War began. Syria attempted to bomb the oil refineries and the West Bank. Syrian artillery bombarded the Israeli forces in eastern Galilee and the villages in the Huleh Valley close to the Golan Heights. Israel gained control of the Golan Heights on June 10, 1967. For nineteen years, the Israelis were provoked by Syria. However, six years later in a surprise attack on Yon Kippur, the Syrians overran the Golan Heights before being repulsed by the Israeli counter attacks.

Moshe Dayan was the defense minister during the Six Day War. He was also instrumental as the commander of the Jerusalem front in the 1948 Arab-Israeli War. One day Moshe Dayan decided to take an unscheduled tour of the kibbutzes in the Hula Valley. Along the road he noticed a little boy marching back and forth mimicking a soldier. Dayan directed his driver to pull over.

"What is your name?" Dayan asked the boy.

"I am Gilad," he replied as he continued to march.

"Do you know who I am?" Dayan replied.

The little boy looked at him. "No sir I do not know. Who are you?"

Gilad's father, who was tending to his goats, approached them. "Mr. Dayan, it is a pleasure to meet you. Come with me to my modest home where my wife will make us lunch."

"No, thank you, sir, but I must be on my way."

Gilad, being a precocious child, was curious about Dayan's appearance. "Why do you have a patch over your eye?"

"Gilad, do not be rude. Say you are sorry to Mr. Dayan."

"That is all right. No need to scold your son. I lost the sight of my eye in combat helping the British fighting against the French in Syria in the year 1941. I just had to stop and say what a fine little boy you are."

Gilad poked his chest proudly with his thumb. "When I grow up I want to be a soldier and fight all the enemies of Israel."

Dayan smiled then patted Gilad's head. "Well, if I am still alive, I will make darn sure to see it comes true."

The 1972 Munich Olympics brought about another dark chapter of the hatred between Israel and their Arab neighbors. Palestinian terrorists gained access into the Olympic Village and quickly located where the Israeli athletes were. They castrated an athlete who was a fencer and tortured several others. The German police and members of the army arrived as the terrorists known as Black September held the hostages in their rooms. The terrorists demanded the release of political prisoners in exchange for the Israeli athlete's freedom. They also wanted an airplane to be fueled and ready to take off so that they could escape jurisdiction.

The negotiations continued as the terrorists waved flags from the windows, defying to be shot by snipers while they held guns to the heads of their captives. Transportation was arranged as the heavily armed Palestinian terrorists briskly hustled the Israeli athletes into the vehicles. Once they arrived at the airport, German snipers took out the terrorists, but unfortunately the Israeli captives were killed.

Golda Meir was incensed by what happened in Munich. So she orchestrated a covert operation dubbed Wrath of God – Operation Bayonet (Kidon) to assassinate the leader of the September Terrorists. The Mossad was the elite team that would eventually track down those who were responsible.

One of the members of the Mossad was that same little boy who Moshe Dayan had encountered. Gilad Habbib, the future father of Ziva and Ari.

9

The Turning Stone Resort and Casino in Verona is close to an airport, easy access for the high rollers better known as the Whales. But most of the visitors drive or take a bus. There are several hundred guestrooms with full service amenities to satisfy your every whim. There is valet parking and roundtrip shuttle to the airport.

The Turning Stone was developed from muddy cornfields into a mega complex that helped create over a thousand jobs. Most of those employed are members of the Oneida Nation. Malachi Eaglefeather is in charge of security, making sure that there are no breeches when it comes to safety on the Turning Stone property. Malachi makes it a point to review the latest videos of the surveillance cameras before he begins his rounds throughout the casino.

One of the customers in particular has caught his eye. He slowed the video down, then clicked to zoom in for a closer look. Sure enough, it is Morgan Fletcher. Malachi jots down the time displayed on the video. With that information, Malachi contacted the valet parking manager to find out if Fletcher came to the casino alone or with someone.

Later on, Malachi contacted Sheriff Fast and told him about Fletcher paying a visit to the casino. Collectively they concluded that perhaps Fletcher was doubling back to the scene of the crime where Morosco's body was found to make sure there wasn't any trace of evidence left behind which could tie him to the murder.

"Say, Malachi, do you have the make of the car? Better yet, how about the license plate? I could run it through the DMV database and see what they come up with."

"Thanks, Sheriff. I will have to get back to you later … there seems to be a problem with one of the high rollers who is causing a scene in the casino."

"Sure, take your time. I'll speak to you later."

Malachi straps on his holster and gun, then slips on his jacket to conceal the weapon. The blackjack dealer who is a friend of Malachi's explains to him that the gambler was being belligerent after losing most of his chips. Malachi confronts the man who is in his late 60's. He is heavyset and wearing a sweat suit. He is seated in a handicapped scooter with a portable oxygen tank and a plastic tube in his nose.

"What seems to be the matter sir?" Malachi asked him.

"Oh, if it isn't Geronimo himself," the man remarked rudely. "I was robbed."

"Robbed, sir, by whom?"

"By the dealer, that's who. I saw him palming the cards. Yup, I can spot a card cheater for sure."

"Sir, I can assure you the casino is not out to cheat you or any of our guests. Now if you would just follow me, I will be more than happy to make your stay with Turning Stone a more pleasant experience."

Malachi has the expertise to defuse a situation before it gets out of hand. The old man collects the remainder of his chips and deposits them in the basket of the scooter, then trails Malachi to the cashier. Malachi tells the cashier to give the man a coupon for a free complimentary all-you-can-eat buffet plus a night's stay in one of the posh penthouse suites.

"I hope that this will make up for any inconvenience that occurred today."

The old man is delighted as he scoots away.

"He's one bad mama jamma," Malachi said to the cashier.

"You do know that he's tried this before," the cashier replied.

"I know, but look at him, he's living on borrowed time. He'll probably go back to some trailer park or assisted living facility and brag to anyone who will listen to how he pulled a fast one on the redskins at their casino."

Later in the day Malachi called the sheriff. "The vehicle is a dark blue Cadillac Escalade with a NY tag."

Jasper checked the plate in the DMV database. It turned out to be a rental. He related this to Malachi. Jasper then placed a call to the rental company.

The auto rep entered the information and came up with a hit. "Here it is, Sheriff. The vehicle was rented to a Nicodemus Morosco. He paid with a credit card."

Jasper, to say the least, is taken aback. "One other question, has it been returned?"

"Not yet, Sheriff. Will there be anything else?"

"No, that's it thanks."

So now what? Jasper ponders. If the black suspect is driving the vehicle, maybe the built-in GPS could locate his whereabouts, but easier said than done. He doesn't have the time to drop all the other cases on his desk, but this one is a murder case. Murders seldom occur in his jurisdiction. It pesters him that he cannot come up with any evidence at the crime scene. And why was Morosco dumped in the woods? If it was a professional hit by the mob, they did a lousy job. Nope, this was probably done in haste. Maybe when Malachi encountered them, they figured the Indian was onto them. Maybe just maybe, they thought he would call the cops so they had to take out Morosco ASAP. Sooner or later they'll make a mistake and we'll get them.

The bulldog is snoring in the corner near the electric heater. "C'mon, Buford, it's time for you to take me for a walk."

10

Karen Stone has taken a turn for the better. Dr. Simon is at her bedside when she opened her eyes. "How are you feeling?" he asked her.

Karen looked at him, then at the foot of her bed. She doesn't know where she is. "Where am I?"

"You are in the hospital. I am Dr. Simon. You were seriously injured in your home."

Karen noticed the needle in her hand, which is attached to a plastic tube, connected to an IV filled with saline solution. "How ... where is my husband Herb? Is he okay?"

Dr. Simon held her hand. "You had a near-death experience. It was touch and go. You are lucky to be alive."

"When can I go home?"

"You are still weak. When your vital signs are back to normal, then you will be released. But until then, you have to get your strength back. After all the trauma you went through, your fetus is healthy I'm pleased to report."

Karen propped herself up in the bed to get comfortable. "Did you say fetus, doctor?"

"Yes, that is what I said. You are in first trimester and even though you lost a considerable amount of blood, it apparently didn't affect the fetus. You must surely have a guardian angel watching over you."

"My parents told me I have a mensch protecting me. Does my husband know that he will be a father?"

"Mrs. Fishman, how can I say this without being prejudice ... your husband hasn't been around to visit since you were admitted. I suspect he had something to do with your injury."

Karen cannot believe what she is hearing. "No, doctor, you've got him all wrong. Herb adores me; he is a good man. How could you say such a thing?" Her eyes are covered in tears.

"Would you like me to contact your family, Mrs. Fishman? I bet they would love to hear your voice."

He moved the phone next to her so she could call her mother. Sylvia was over the moon to hear her daughter's voice once again. She was beside herself wanting to tell Milt the good news. Her husband has been patiently waiting to see the outcome of Karen's condition because he has a score to settle with his son-in-law.

Shortly after dinner he decided to pay Shelly Fishman a visit. Fishman has a kosher deli down by the Brooklyn Bridge. Along for the ride with the doctor were Sid and Fletcher.

They bide their time until the last customer leaves the store. They exit the car and walk up to the front door of the deli. They try to enter but it is locked. Sid pounds on the window to get Shelly's attention. He is in the back room so he ordered his butcher to tell whoever it is that they are closed and to come back tomorrow. Well, before you know it, they have forced the butcher to open the door. When he spotted the gun in Fletcher's hand, the butcher unlocked the door. Sid told him to get lost and out the shop he darted, the bloody apron still wrapped around him.

Shelly switched off the light in the back room, then turned around expecting to see his butcher, but instead there are three set of eyes staring at him who are definitely not last-minute shopping for kosher meats.

Shelly's face is white as a roll of butcher paper. His hands are shaking, so he stuffed them inside the pockets of his pants.

"Milton, what a surprise. What brings you here this hour of the night?"

Sid stepped up to him and grabbed him by his shirt collar. Through clenched teeth he asked, "Where's Herb? Where the hell is he?"

"I don't know ... we haven't seen him."

Sid pinned him to the wall that had meat hooks hanging on a rack. "Don't give me that crap. My sister almost died because of him. You know it; your old lady knows it. So for the last time, where the hell is he?"

"I swear by the beards of Moses and Abraham, I do not know his whereabouts." Shelly looked at Milt for leniency. "Milton, for the love of Jehovah, help me. I am telling you the truth. Herb was here right after he took Brenda's cash and credit cards. He wanted me to help him out, but I told Herb to turn himself in."

Milt slides a chair away from the table in the corner of the store, then sat down. He unbuttoned his cashmere overcoat, pulled out a cigar and struck a match. "You know something, Shelly? Everybody always raves about your meats. You have the freshest chickens, the top choice of beef, and the cold cuts are to die for."

The doctor flicked the cigar ashes onto the sawdust floor, then wiped his lap with the back of his hand. He stood up, and then walked behind the meat counter. He flipped the switch to activate the meat slicer. The razor sharp circular blade swiftly turned. The neon lights in the front window are reflected on the stainless steel cutting edge. Stone gestures to Fletcher to lower the shades on the door and window.

Stone's cigar is tossed into the sink that has yet to be cleaned. It still has remnants of animal parts, fish gills and guts, chicken feathers, and blood. Stone pulled off a sheet of the butcher paper from the roll and slid it next to the slicer. "You know what you are, Shelly? You are a kolboynick, a know-it-all. Or so they say. To which I say, you are nothing more than a drek, a worthless piece of dust. You tell me you have no idea where Herbie is and I am supposed to take your word and believe you? What do you take me for, Shelly? Do I look like a schmuck to you?"

"No, Milton, never. I respect you, always have. Everybody knows Dr. Stone. I tell all my customers if you're sick go to your office to get well."

Fletcher slides open the door of the deli case where trays of fresh-cut poultry, fish, and meat are displayed.

Shelly's eyes dart back and forth. "Take whatever you want. It's on the house."

Fletcher slides the door closed.

The doctor buttons up the overcoat, pats Shelly's cheeks with his hands, then slowly walks to the front door. "I'll be in the car. Don't be too long. And don't forget the knishes."

11

Connor O'Roarke, the day bartender at the Two Timer's, had just arrived to open the joint when he heard a car alarm. He paid it no mind as it blended in with the rest of the constant blare out in the street. But after more than fifteen minutes he threw the bar towel over his shoulder, then stepped outside to investigate. The car alarm was not coming from the street but behind the bar in the common alleyway. Connor unlocked the back door to find an SUV with the alarm wailing and the lights flashing.

As he got closer to the vehicle, a patrol car from the 61st Precinct pulled up behind the bar. The cop attempted to open the locked doors to the SUV. Seated behind the wheel is the driver with a brown shopping bag over his head. The cop pulled out his slim metal flashlight, rapped it on the window to get the drivers attention. There is no response from the driver. The cop then breaks the driver's door window. There is no movement by the driver, so the cop removes the brown shopping bag. The man has no face. It has been sliced down to the bone. The cop raced back to his car and called for an ambulance.

Soon a crowd began to gather around the grisly scene. Within minutes detectives Dobbs and Pickett arrive to assess the situation. A tow truck is dispatched to take away the vehicle. Once the evidence had been gathered, the detectives found out that the deceased is

Shelly Fishman and that the SUV is a Cadillac Escalade leased to Nick Morosco.

The medical examiner has determined that Fishman's face was hacked off by a very sharp object, possibly a meat slicer. "Hey, Chuck, what are the odds that the guy who was knocked off in the woods upstate would have his rental wheels parked right across the street where he lived?"

"Not only that, Bruce, but he's already dead and another stiff was driving in his place. Not for nothing but we got a serial killer on the loose. Both killings have to be connected."

As the detectives continued to probe for a possible link between Morosco and Fishman they come to a dead end. "There has to be somebody who knew them, something to put them in a place at the same time."

"We have a Jewish kosher deli owner and a wannabe guinea dope pusher offed more than likely by the same guy. "

"Did the forensic team dust the Caddy for prints?"

"That they did, Bruce, from bumper to bumper. Came up clean as a whistle, as if a surgeon was about to perform an operation. It was sterile. Only Fishman's DNA turned up."

In accordance with the Jewish orthodox tradition, the body of Shelly Fishman was laid to rest within 24 hours. A temporary structure made of wood is placed in the backyard where Brenda will sit in Shiva. All of the mirrors in the house have been covered out of respect for the bereaved. Brenda and her extended family greet neighbor's friends and loyal customers who frequented the deli. Noticeably absent was the Stone family. It did not go unnoticed as their names were more than once mentioned to Brenda. She would reply that her daughter-in-law was home and Sylvia and Milt were helping her out.

However, to everyone's amazement, who was it that should appear but Herb? He was all disheveled, his hair was uncombed and dirty, the eyes were bloodshot, his clothes were filthy, and his body odor reeked. Brenda dropped her glass filled with red wine. Then she raced into the kitchen. anticipating that her son would resort to taking out his anger on her. But that was not the case. Instead, he worked his way through the crowded living room, shaking hands to those who were paying their respects.

He confronted his mother at the kitchen table. "I'm sorry, mom. I was desperate when I hurt you."

Brenda is incredulous. "You have no idea how much you hurt me, no idea! Now look at what happened. Your father is dead. I ask you, are you the reason why? My Shelly loved everyone, he didn't have a bad bone in his body. All of this happened because of what you did to your wife? I possess a women's intellect plus as a wife and mother. I smell something that isn't kosher." Herb smells to high heaven. "Go take a shower and scrub yourself clean."

Meanwhile at the Stone residence, the news of Shelly's death is mixed with emotions. Sylvia wanted to pay her respects, but Milt will not let her attend.

"Serves them right, mom. Look at what their son did to Karen," Sid told her.

"Now you don't know that, son. Until I can hear from Karen exactly what happened to her, I will reserve judgement for your brother-in-law."

The doctor grabbed his hat, coat, and the black medical bag, then departed. He needed to pay a visit to Sweet Magnolia's place for some long and desperately needed horizontal pleasure time.

12

Finn McCoole grew up in one of the poorest areas of Belfast where the British Army patrolled the streets keeping watch on the rebels of Sein Fein. One day outside the Europa Hotel a car bomb exploded at the curb. The blast blew out the windows of the hotel, killing four and injuring seven. The intended target, a Member of Parliament, escaped a certain death if not for being detained stuck inside the elevator. Finn McCoole was the bomber who made a hasty getaway, then set sail to New York.

He bounced around the city working odd jobs off the books until one day he bumped into Declan McDermit, a fellow Irishman. Declan, short and stocky, is an amateur boxer who makes a living pushing drugs. Together with McCoole, they live in an apartment in Woodside across the street from Donovan's Pub. It is located on Roosevelt Avenue where the El rumbles above.

Together they pooled their money and started to attract customers who were in need of a fix. Fentanyl was the drug of choice, sold in tiny packets with the street names Apache, China Girl, China White, Dance Fever, Friend, Goodfellas, Jackpot, Murder8, TNT, Tango and Cash. Finn and Declan would hit the local bars and strip clubs to make the deals.

Living in the apartment nearby is Maureen Flynn, a cute little redhead with hazel eyes, who is an RN at Coney Island Hospital. Declan and Finn are indeed interested, but she is involved with a detective in Brooklyn, a cop named Bruce Pickett. Helping to distribute the drugs is Tootsie Snow, a brunette definitely easy on the eyes, but with a brain for business. A close friend of Maureen is Joyce Owens, who is into physical fitness. She just aced the firefighters test at the Academy and has been assigned to a hook-and-ladder house in Red Hook.

So while Finn had his contacts and the business began to prosper, another partner would soon come into play. One night while Maureen was working her shift at the hospital, she met Dr. Milton Stone. They made the rounds on the ward and for some unknown reason Milton gave Maureen his cell phone number.

"If you ever need something to make you feel better, you know a quick pick-me-up, give me a call." The doctor stepped into the elevator as the door closed.

Maureen shook her head, but tucked his business card into her pocket. Throughout the rest of her shift, she cannot shake the audacity of the doctor. It lingered with her even when Bruce picked her up outside the hospital. She told him all about it.

He just smiled while he drove her to his place. "Hey, the doctor's probably horny. His old lady, I bet, is fat and couldn't care less about getting laid. So he sees you're a hot-lookin' nurse, doesn't see a ring on your finger, and assumes you're available."

Maureen punches him in the arm. "Men! All you ever think about is sex, sex, sex."

"And if we didn't what would all the women have to talk about?"

They arrive at his place when his cellphone rang. He let Maureen out of the car, reminding her to take the keys to the apartment. "Sorry, babe, but I have to go. There has been another murder. I have to respond to right away. I'll call you if I get a chance."

"I'll be waiting for you. Kiss kiss," Maureen said as she waved goodbye.

The detective puts the car in Drive, then peeled out down the street. By the time he arrives, Chuck Dobbs has taken charge of the scene. A yellow tape emblazoned with DO NOT CROSS CRIME SCENE is whipping in the night air. In the back alley, just off Kings Highway, is a white sheet covering a body.

"Who called it in?" Dobbs asked the responding officer.

"It was Mrs. Gold. According to her, she heard a woman screaming in the rear of the building."

"Did she see who attacked her?"

"No, detective, sorry to say."

Pickett and Dobbs crouch down. Pickett pulled back the sheet to view the body. "Hey, isn't this the barfly we talked to about Nick Morosco?"

"You know, Chuck, I think you're right." There are puncture wounds to her chest and arms. "Looks like, she put up one hell of a fight for her life."

"Do you think there's a connection between the murders?"

"Maybe, you can never tell."

There is the strong smell of alcohol on the body and her shopping cart is twisted and bent nearby. The detectives decide to pay a visit to the Two Timer's bar across the street. The night bartender is Buster Coogan. He is short and heavy-set. Sporting a stubby beard, he has a broken nose and a scar on his chin. Needless to say, he is in no mood to talk with them. He is busy working the taps refilling the regular's glasses.

On the television screen directly above the bar the station is tuned in to President Trump declaring war on the opioid epidemic. "Trumps a chump" one of the drunks commented as he lit up another cigarette.

Dobbs and Pickett flash their badges as they stand at the bar.

"We're here investigating the murder of Mary Dunham that took place not far from here" Dobbs told him.

"Yeah so?" Coogan replied in his heavy Irish brogue. "What's that got to do with me?"

To which Pickett slams his hand hard on the bar. "She was a regular in this dive. She had a name and now she's DEAD. She knew Nick Morosco, so don't tell us you never heard of him."

"Look, all I do is serve the customers. I don't ask for their name, where they live, or the last time they got humped. The less I know the better. When you keep your pie hole shut, you got nobody getting into your life, if you know what I mean?"

"C'mon, Bruce, we're wasting our time talkin' to this Irish prick."

13

Come early November, once the trees of green have changed into spectacular colors of red orange and brown, most of the tourists are gone. Sure, there might be a group of hunters prowling through the woods in search of deer or bear but that is far and in between. For Jasper this is the time of the year he anticipates. He is passionate when it comes to fly-fishing. He'll wake up way before dawn, load up his truck, and take off to a secluded spot that few know about. He could cast his line in Esopus Creek, but it is where the kids go tubing. Not the place for him. Nope, Jasper enjoys the solitude. Holly, his wife, understands that every man needs to get away to clear his head about matters that clutter one's life.

Jasper pulls on his waders and zips up the windbreaker. The weather forecast is calling for rain and a dip in the temperature. Jasper ties one of his fishing lures to the line, straps on the fishing net over his shoulder, then proceeds down to the creek. The rocks are slippery underfoot as tiny rivulets of the swift current converge to form swift sets of rapids. Jasper casts the line out into the stream with a flick of the wrist. The lure skims the surface on the water as Jasper manipulates a subtle movement to attract the fish.

Sure enough, he has a bite. Jasper yanks the rod, then commences to reel it in. The speckled trout glimmers in the sunlight that breaks through the leafy branches. Jasper's rod is bent like an upside down large letter U. The fish is determined to survive another day. Jasper gives the fish time to tire itself out. Then, ever so gently, he allows the fish to swim into the net. Jasper removes the hook from the trout's mouth. He holds the fish in his hands to admire the size and color. Then he lets it go back into the stream.

From the top pocket of his bib overalls he pulls out a corncob pipe, a tobacco pouch, and a box of matches. Jasper takes a break from fishing to light up the pipe. There is a rustling of fallen leaves on the ground of an approaching animal. Jasper left his weapon back in the truck so he only has his bare hands to defend himself. Out from the woods emerges Malachi. Jasper is relieved to know that it is his friend.

"How the hell did you know where to find me?"

"A good Indian tracker has many ways to find what they seek."

"Holly told you where I'd be."

"How did you know that?"

"A good sheriff has many ways to figure out a mystery, but leave it to a wife to keep a secret it's not going to happen."

They find a spot to sit. Malachi unscrews the cap of his thermos filled with hot coffee and shares it with Jasper. Jasper taps the ashes from the corncob, then commences to refill the bowl with tobacco.

"That's going to kill you, Jasper, if you keep it up."

Jasper lights the pipe filled with the tobacco. "We only got so much time on this land so I might as well enjoy it. Hell, everybody has something in their lives that takes them down an uncharted stream."

"Just like the fish, Jasper."

"Exactly, just like the fish they spawn upstream, then once they are fully grown, they test the waters by swimming downstream hoping to find the perfect mate."

"Then they get hooked and it's all over for them."

"Maybe yes, maybe no. It all depends on the angler. Me, I just let them go. I mean, what's the point in keeping them? Sure, a pan-fried trout is mighty tasty, but I'd rather let them do what the Good Lord had intended them to do. Procreate so that future schools will have the opportunity to swim in the streams."

"Fishing means a lot to you, Jasper."

"That it does. It is more than a hobby. It lets me escape; it allows me to appreciate what I take for granted."

"How is that so, Jasper?"

"Well," he takes a puff on the pipe, "I see the tourists trampin' in the woods outfitted in LL Bean, Cabela's, and the Bass outfits. Some even have the price tags attached. I reckon they'll return them soon after they get back to the city. They haven't a clue about the outdoor life. So they take their cellphones and snap their selfies, post it on their social media sites for all to see. Then they count how many hits they got. Who the hell cares?"

Malachi empties the remains of the coffee from the thermos.

"So what brings you here, Malachi, that could not wait?"

"There's trouble on the res."

"How is that so, friend of mine?"

"Somebody is pushing dope and a few of the kids are being admitted to the hospital after an OD."

"It is an epidemic, for sure. We had drugs when I was a kid, but not like this. It is so cheap and easy to get."

"There was always peyote on the res, but nobody died from smoking it."

They return to their trucks, and drive down the road toward Chirp. As they near Lucy's Truck Stop Diner, Jasper spots a state trooper that he knows. He pulls into the gravel parking lot; Malachi follows him there. Jasper

shakes hands with Brody Pence. Brody is assigned to K
Troop, an undercover team of troopers. Pence is dressed
in camouflage pants, a black hoodie, and Carhart boots.
He has a ruddy complexion a full beard a pair of
diamond studs adorn his ears. Jasper introduces
Malachi to Brody.

"How's it going?" Brody asked Jasper.

"Good and how about, yourself?"

"It's crazy up here. Homegrown meth labs are
cooking some bad shit and pushin' their poison mostly
to kids. They have no idea what they're putting into their
bodies."

Jasper mentions the case he's working on. "Ever
heard of a drug dealer, Nick Morosco?"

"Nah, never heard of him. Who is he?"

"His body was dumped in the woods at
Peekamoose."

"That was that dude? Huh, so you caught the case,
Sheriff?" "

Yup and ... Malachi, well, you tell him about what
you saw at the casino."

Malachi related to Brody about the video that
captured the image of Morgan Fletcher and the Cadillac
Escalade. The trooper's cellphone rings; it is from the
lead detective on his team. "I have to go. It's been good
seeing you, Jasper. Nice meeting you, Malachi."

"Take care, Brody. Say, do you still got that Harley?"

"Sure do, I drive it whenever I get the chance."

"That's one sweet ride," Malachi remarked. "I had a
knucklehead a few years ago, but I took one too many
spills. Figured the odds were stacked against me from
getting busted up flying down the road."

"Hey you only live once. Adios."

14

As the final days of November are fast approaching, the annual Macy's Thanksgiving Day Parade preparations are in full swing. The mayor and the police commissioner have assured the public that the NYPD will make sure that the parade will be safe from any act of terrorism. All of the 125 parking garages will be watched as well as an army of snipers on rooftops as an added layer of protection. Specially trained canines will be on hand to detect trace amounts of explosive particles on any person carrying materials to make a bomb. All of the members of the NYPD will be on high alert until after the New Year's Eve Celebration in Times Square.

Ari Habbib is a master of disguises and is now in New York. Inside the apartment in Alley Pond Park, Ali dons a short black woman's wig. He applies makeup to his face, attaches fake finger tips to his nails, then checks his image in the bathroom mirror. Inside the hall closet is a large Macy's shopping bag. Hanging on the hook is a Santa Claus outfit with a white beard and wig. Last but not least is a free standing plastic red-and-white candy cane. It is filled with ball bearings marble and carpet nails.

The terrorist exits the apartment toting the bag with the Santa suit and the improvised bomb. He walks to the corner of Cloverdale Boulevard and Union Turnpike where he will board the Q46 bus. Ali will depart the bus at Queens Boulevard and then descend down to the subway entrance where he will take the F train to 34th Herald Square and 6th Avenue. Once he arrives, he will proceed to 151 West 34th where the Macy's Department Store is located.

The Thanksgiving Day Parade is underway as the large inflatable helium balloons fill the air. Marching bands from all over the country in colorful costumes brave the chilly morning in hopes of being seen on television. There is a heavy police presence on the sidewalks as Habbib negotiates ever so closer to the main entrance of Macy's. He hesitates for a split second, then decides it is better to enter one of the side doors where security might be lacking. There are two heavily armed NYPD cops positioned at the door as he approaches. Habbib smiles at them, knowing full well the female disguise is convincing. They allow him to pass.

Once he is inside the store, he locates the nearest restrooms. He is about to enter the men's room, then pivots to the ladies room. He quickly closes the bathroom stall door and gets to work. He removes the wig the fake nails and makeup. Habbib dons the Santa Claus disguise, places all the female items into the shopping bag then, exits the restroom. Holding the candy cane in one hand and the shopping bag in the other, he walks through the store to the official Santa Claus display.

Ari Habbib places the candy cane as close as possible to the red velvet rope at the entrance to Santa's Workshop. Ari then places the Macy's shopping bag over his shoulder and exits the store. He could have easily placed the bag into a trash receptacle, but thought about a better option. He steps outside and feels the cold brisk air on his face. He is not used to a cold winter's day in New York. Most of his life was spent in the Middle East and France.

Ari's father Gilad sent him to Paris after he graduated from high school in Jerusalem. He became friends with a Palestinian girl who at first would not give him the time of day. But as it became obvious that Ari was attracted to her, she relented and they moved in together. Shalimar Saddiq —her eyes and hair are dark brown. She dresses in the traditional hajib and attire. She is fluent in Hebrew, Farsi, French, and English. She introduced Ari to a radical group on the college campus. They showed to him anti-Israeli videos of what the Arabs had to endure during the Six Day War. At first Ari was defensive. He proclaimed to them that his father was a member of the Mossad who assassinated the Palestinians who were responsible for the attack on the Munich Olympics. The confrontations continued as if he and Shalimar were seated at a chess table pitted against each other.

Suddenly, there is a large noise out in the street. One of the balloons in the parade, Big Bird from Sesame Street, has been punctured in the beak. The balloon springing a leak brings Ari back from his deep thoughts of the past. Some of the children in the crowd wave to him and smile. Reluctantly, he chuckles and shouts: "Ho! Ho! Ho!"

Ari makes his way back to the subway station, where he ditches the Macy's shopping bag. The subway platform is packed as he is jostled closer to a dirty upright stanchion. The F train arrives and as the passengers exit he manages to squeeze into the subway car just as the doors are about to close. He rolls back his sleeve to check the time on his wristwatch. Inside his pants pocket is an untraceable burner phone. He waits until the train stops at 23rd and Eli, then makes the call to the bomb that ignites the contents of the candy cane.

What only a few seconds ago was a happy holiday treat to so many, now Macy's has been transformed into a killing field. Women and children are blown to bits; the store Santa is nothing more than body parts. Christmas decorations fill the air amid the acrid smell of smoldering flesh. The blast has temporarily deafened the bystanders. There are shards of glass from the display cases; mannequins outfitted in various clothing are ablaze. The fire sprinklers are showering the entire store in conjunction with the fire alarms.

Macy's has become a war zone that no one was prepared for. Life in the Big Apple has taken a serious hit, now added to the list of 9/11 and the Boston Marathon Bombing.

Ali Habbib returns to this apartment where he bumps into his neighbor, Joyce Owens. She is all set to take a jog up to Cunningham Park.

"Well, aren't you in the festive occasion, all decked out as Santa," she said.

"Have you been a good girl this year?"

Joyce wets her lips with her tongue, then whispers into his ear. "That's for me to know and for Santa to find out." She plants a kiss on his cheek, and then trots off down the steps. He watches her as she continues to jog down the street. "Fools all of them! These infidels have no idea what is in store for them. Today is just the beginning."

A throng of cops, ATF, and FBI converge upon the scene of the bombing. The governor, mayor, and the police commissioner address the media at One Police Plaza. They might as well be talking heads commenting on the horrific event. "It is too early to say whether this has been an act of terrorism or perhaps a random act of violence. But whoever is responsible, if you are watching this, we will not be satisfied until you are caught and prosecuted. Until that time, New Yorkers, go about your everyday routine. Do not despair. We will be collecting evidence in the interim. It is all hands on deck."

A reporter shouts from the gaggle covering the news event: "Mayor, what you have said is all well and good, but have you got anything to say to the victims and their families?"

The governor steps in front of the mayor to make a statement. "We will cover all expenses. The State of New York will be contacting the president, who has already reached out to us. President Trump and the Democrats haven't seen eye to eye since his inauguration, but on this tragedy we are all on the same team."

15

Teddy Stone is walking home from Yeshiva when he passes the public school playground where a rowdy group of blacks are playing basketball. One of them spots Teddy and shouts to him. "Hey, Jew boy, have you got game?"

Teddy continues to walk, but at a faster clip.

"C'mon, join us. Our blackness won't rub off on you," one of the others remarks.

When Teddy arrives at the corner, the traffic light turns to red, so that he cannot cross over to the other side of busy Surf Avenue. He decides to make a mad dash for fear of being bullied by the blacks. He darts into the oncoming traffic and narrowly avoids being hit by a city bus. He loses his yarmulke in the process. Better that than his life. When he arrives home, he remarks to Sylvia that he wants to take up Kung Fu.

"Kung Fu? Now why in heaven's sake, my son? Teddy, you are a gentle little boy who will one day become a respected rabbi in the community."

"Poppa wants me to work with Sid and Mr. McCoole."

Sylvia has a look of surprise on her face. "Oh, he does, does he? He has already molded Sid into some kind of wannabe gangster; he'll not take you as well."

"Momma, I want to take karate lessons at Tiger Shulman's. Some of the students at yeshiva are enrolled. The neighborhood is changing. A lot of blacks are moving in and I want to be able to defend myself."

Sylvia is in her bathrobe with a towel wrapped around her wet hair. She sorts out the laundry to be washed and tells Teddy that their conversation is far from over in regards to the art of self-defense.

Karen's face is still puffy around her eyes. She will need extensive surgery to mend her broken cheekbones. She will also need dental implants to fill in for her missing teeth that were knocked out by Herb. For the time being, Karen must use a straw to enable her to eat.

At the dinner table the Stones are a family in turmoil as the layers slowly peel away. The bitterness between husband and wife is evident as Sylvia suspects Milt of stepping out on her. As they pass the food, Sylvia lets it all out. "I want a divorce. Enough is enough. It has been going on far too long. I tried to keep it from the children, but now they are all grown up. I want to be happy in my old age. Look at our daughter, just look at her!"

Milt ignores her as he cuts the loaf of bread. "We've been through this before. You can't have a divorce unless I say so. So there is no get (divorce) for you. End of discussion."

Sylvia shakes her head in frustration.

"So, Poppa, I was thinking about taking karate lessons. Momma said to ask you if it's okay."

"Sure, why not? It is a good thing for a man to know how to defend himself."

"He'll only get hurt you'll see. The bullies that go to those places prey on the weak kids."

"Ma, he needs to be able to stand up and be a man. Look at me, I work out lift weights to keep in shape. I could tell him how to box, show him a couple of moves," said Sid.

"Has anyone heard from Herb?" Karen asked through her clenched teeth.

Sid slams down his knife and fork in anger. "Sis, forget about him. He's the reason why you are in the shape you're in. If I ever see that son-of-a-bitch ..."

Milt cuts him off. "I don't want to hear his name or for that matter any of the Fishman's. To me, they are all dead to me."

Sylvia is stunned. "How could you say that? Poor Shelly's body is not cold in the grave and yet you are filled with hate. I do not know you anymore. Where is the Milton I once married?"

"He left a long time ago. I am a different person. I do what has to be done to protect the family."

Karen is experiencing cramps, so she and Sylvia go into the bathroom. The house phone rings Milt tells Sid to answer it. The caller is Finn McCoole.

"Tell yer old man the package he ordered has been delivered."

"Thanks. He'll be happy to hear the good news."

Milt takes Sid with him in the car driven by Fletcher. They arrive at the docks in Red Hook where Finn McCoole is waiting for them. Milt lowers the rear window of the car as the Irishman leans in. "It's all set. The package passed through customs. So now all you have to do is pay the bill."

"Thanks. So which vessel is it?" Milt asks as he takes in the ships that are moored to the docks.

Finn is tentative as his eyes dart side-to-side. He points to a red tanker ship from Palermo, Sicily. The gangplank is all lit up with bright lights. "All you have to do is meet the guy up on the main deck. Simple as that."

Doctor Stone and Sid exit the car while Fletcher opens the trunk and removes an attaché case filled with cash. The three of them climb the gangplank while McCoole watches them from the dock. When they reach the main deck, they meet a gang of stevedores and longshoremen who are standing next to a wooden crate marked FRAGILE CONTENTS HANDLE WITH CARE. On the main deck are cargo nets, grappling hooks, and various boxes of cargo. The top of the crate is pried open by the men. They remove the straw packaging to reveal a metal box wrapped in shrink-wrap. A large sharp knife cuts through the wrapping, then the metal box is opened. Inside the box are four large wheels of imported cheese.

"Pop, this is what we came for?"

"No, but what is inside of them." He takes the knife and carves a hole in the middle of the cheese wheel and removes the wedge. In the middle of the cheese is a white substance. The doctor scoops it with the nail of his pinkie finger then samples it on the tip of his tongue. It is pure opium. He is satisfied with the product so the deal is made. The transfer of cash for the drugs goes off without a hitch. Each wheel of cheese contains a kilo of pure opium. Not since the French Connection has a shipment of drugs to New York slipped by undetected. Once the opium is cut it will be distributed to the bars run by McCoole and up in Harlem courtesy of Belinda Bellows. It is just a matter of time until the doctor will be filling prescriptions for the majority of the junkies in the state of New York. There will be enough to go around so that the Turning Stone Casino will be fixing to deal with Stone.

16

Inside the 61st Precinct, Capt. Millwood is addressing his subordinates. "I don't have to tell you how much I want this low-life scum bucket who planted that bomb in Macy's to be nabbed by the NYPD. Our shit-for-brains mayor and the politically correct governor can't or won't say it was an act orchestrated by Islamic terrorists. To which I say, call it as it is. The makings of ISIS are all over this. So I need your help to put the pressure on all of your confidential informants. Somebody must have seen something or heard something. The latest update so far is that there are numerous casualties, kids missing arms and legs, men and women undergoing surgery and fighting for their lives to survive. Five are deceased including Santa Claus. He was a seasonal worker, a veteran down on his luck living out on the streets. I don't know how this prick managed to get into the store undetected. Right now, the feds are viewing the security tapes of Macy's. Hopefully a suspect will be spotted that can be profiled and proceed into a lead for us. Other than that, it's business as usual. Be safe out there. Have one another's back. That is all for now."

Pickett and Dobbs check the duty roster to see where Millwood wants them for their shift. The recent murder of Mary Dunham has taken a turn. Her credit card has been used at a bodega on Flatbush Avenue. The detectives take a drive over to the store. The owner who hardly speaks a word of English is fearful of the cops because he is an illegal immigrant from Mexico.

"Look, we don't care about your status. All we want to know is, who used the stolen credit card, comprende?" Dobbs said.

"No, I don't remember."

"You don't remember or you don't want to because you know who it is. What is it, buster?" Pickett demanded from him.

"Some kid, el niño. I don't know his name. He bought a six-pack of beer, cervesa candy, scratch-off tickets, and nacho chips. That's it."

"The kid, was he black, white, Latino, Asian, Arab, or maybe a Jew?" asked Dobbs.

"He was wearing a hoodie and sunglasses. His hands were covered in gloves, black gloves I think."

"Did it ever occur to you that the card wasn't his? There is a woman's name on it and now she is dead and you could be involved by allowing a murderer to get away," Dobbs informed him.

Pickett receives a text message on his cellphone. "We have to go, partner. The card was just used at a Game Stop on Bedford Avenue."

They leave the bodega and make a swift beeline, rushing through red lights as car horns blare and a few middle fingers are raised at their careless driving. They pull up in front of the store and spot a suspect that fits the bodega owner's description. A black teenager is about to cross over to the Ebbets Field Housing apartments when the detectives grab his arms and spin him around.

"Hey, let go of me!"

Dobbs yanks the Game Stop bag from the kid's hand, then pulled out a couple of video games.

"You give them back to me!" the kid demanded.

Pickett pats him down to see if the kid has any concealed weapons. He rifles through the pockets and removes the stolen credit card. "Where did you get this?" Pickett asked him.

"I don't have to tell you nuttin'" the kid replies as a small crowd begins to gather around.

Dobbs slaps the cuffs on him, and then whisks the kid away to the station house. There they put the kid into the interrogation room and let him stew for a while before they are ready to grill him.

"Where were you last Wednesday night?" Dobbs asked him.

"I want a lawyer and you didn't read me my rights."

"Oh right, your Miranda Rights. You have the right to remain silent yada yadda yadda. Now what's your name?"

"Henry Jackson."

"Are you related to Reggie or Bo?"

"Who dat?" The kid crosses his arms and looks up at the ceiling.

"Once again where were you last Wednesday night?"

"I was at your crib bangin' your old lady."

Dobbs gets up to smack him across his face, but Pickett holds him back. "Do you think we're fooling around with you?" he shouts at the kid. "You are in possession of a stolen credit card that belonged to a woman who was murdered last Wednesday night. Right now, you are the main suspect who killed her."

The kid is now scared shitless. "I ain't killed nobody. I ain't like that. All I do is knock offs, you know … takin' stuff that's it."

"Ever heard of the word JOB, asshole? That's what most teens do, they work hard and keep out of trouble," Dobbs told him.

"Maybe in your hood, not mine. Ain't nobody goin' to give a black smartass a job. All the stores are owned by Asians and Jews. What chance have I got?"

"So you just decide that today you're going to rob somebody to get your Air Jordan's, Ray Bans, and the fancy jewelry?" Pickett asked him.

The kid smiles. "Ya'll like my style, check out my bling." He flashes the diamond-studded Rolex. "That's the real thing, not some cheap knockoff."

The interrogation goes back and forth for the next few hours. Then they take a break. Outside in the hall the detectives assess the situation. "You think the kid killed her?"

"My gut tells me no, Chuck. He's a wannabe, a smartass punk."

"So we just cut him loose?"

"Nope we hold him on possession of stolen goods."

"I got a better option and see what he does."

They resume grilling the kid, until finally Pickett tells him that he is going to prison unless he has something to add.

"I got the card from some dude."

"What dude?" asked Dobbs.

"I don't know, just some dude."

"When was this?"

"I don't know. Sometime last week."

"Was it last Wednesday night?"

"I don't know, maybe."

"Look, kid, you have to be specific. If you don't want to get your ass thrown in a cell. There are a lot of lifers who would love to make you their bitch."

"Okay, yeah, it was that night two white dudes were drivin' down Bedford and pulled up alongside of me. The dude in the front seat who wasn't drivin' sold me the card. That's all I know."

"Can you identify them if we showed you some mug shots?"

"I don't know, maybe. They both talked funny."

"Funny like ha ha funny, as a joke?" Pickett said.

"No, like they weren't from here. Had a foreign accent."

"Well, that really narrows it down for us, kid. You really expect us to believe this cock-and-bull story?"

"Listen, I'm tellin' you the truth. These dudes sounded like, you know, like the drunks who get dressed up for the green parade."

"The green parade, you mean the St. Patrick's Day Parade?" asked Dobbs.

"Yeah, that's the one."

"So they come from Ireland. What about the car? What were they driving?"

"It was maybe a Chevy or a Ford, no maybe a Buick. I don't know. I didn't get a look at it. It sure wasn't a high-end ride like the rappers tool around in."

The kid is handed a pen and pad to write down what he has just said. "Sign it with your name, address, and phone number," Pickett said. "You're still on the hook for the stolen goods. If what you say is true and we nail those who killed the woman, we'll tell the DA to give you a pass so that you won't have a record that will follow you wherever you go," Dobbs told him.

After writing it down, the kid bops out into the hall, slides on the Ray Bans and flips the hoodie over his head.

"He'll be back, mark my words. If they aren't selling crack they're ripping off the public. It's just a matter of time before he's back in the system," Bruce surmises.

"So Mary Dunham gets killed in an alley, supposedly by two Micks. What am I missing?"

"Well she knew Morosco. This we know for sure."

"Right. Chuck, and then there was that guy who was found in the Caddy behind the Two Timer's bar."

"Okay, so there are three murders, but just Morosco and Mary knew each other. The other guy was a Jewish deli owner."

"Do you think they might have crossed paths at one time?"

Dobbs snaps his fingers. "The Caddy was rented by Morosco, so there is the connection to all three."

17

Herb Fishman is going stir-crazy staying at his mother's home. So he decides to take the keys and open his father's delicatessen. He unlocked the metal gate, then rolled it up and out of the way. Then he opened the front door. He flipped the switch to turn on the lights, but he stood in the dark. No one has been there since the cops investigated the scene of the crime. Herb knows that there is a safe securely hidden in the meat locker. He opens the thick wooden door, then enters. It reeks to high heaven. Thanks to Brenda for having the electric turned off by Con Ed. Always one to save a buck, Herb said to himself.

Herb covers his mouth and nose with his arm to hide the smell of the rotten meat, poultry, and fish. On the back wall Herb slides a wooden board. Tucked away in a cubbyhole is a metal safe. Where Shelly kept the keys to the store he also had the combination to the safe written on a small piece of paper. Herb turns the dial on the safe clockwise, then counter clockwise, and finally clockwise 31-17-22. The safe is unlocked and inside is a metal cashbox. Herb pulled it out, then opened it. There are deeds to cemetery plots for the family, a piece of faded fabric embroidered with a yellow Jewish star, and a 9mm Glock fully loaded.

Herb tucks the gun into his waistband, then replaced the cashbox inside the safe and moved the wooden board back into place. He then leaves the deli and secures it. Now he feels safe, knowing that he is armed in case he should bump into Sid Stone. Herb arrives back home and decides to call the hospital at Kiryas Joel. The nurse informs him that Karen has been discharged. He then placed a call to their apartment, let it ring a few times until the answering machine picked up. He left no message.

In a rush to judgment, Herb dials up Karen's parent's home phone. It rings twice before Sylvia picks up. "Mrs. Stone? It's me, Herb. Is Karen there? I just called the hospital and our apartment, so I was…"

She cut him off. "Where have you been? You have some nerve calling here. Do you know how close to death Karen was and now she is pregnant?"

"Karen's pregnant? I had no idea."

Karen hears Sylvia raising her voice from her bedroom. "Who are you talking to?" she asked.

"Your good-for-nothing husband, that's who."

"Herbie's on the phone? Oh, let me talk to him."

"I don't think that is a good idea in your condition." Reluctantly she hands her the phone.

"Herbie, how are you?"

He has to compose himself before he speaks to her. "I'm okay … listen, I am so sorry for what I did to you. Can you ever forgive me?"

The fetus kicks inside Karen's womb. "All is forgiven, Herbie. We are all heartbroken over your father's untimely death."

"Thank you. Listen, can I see you? I have a lot to tell you."

Karen takes a moment to reply. She looks around to see if Sylvia is nearby. She is not. "Do not come here, it is not safe. I am scheduled to see my OB-GYN who will check out the baby with an ultrasound. The doctor's office is across the street from the Coney Island Hospital. Meet me there tomorrow at ten sharp."

"I'll be there, Karen. I promise until then, I love you."

Sylvia and Karen spend the next few minutes arguing about Herb. "He better not step foot into this house. You know how bad your brother's temper is."

"Yes, mother, I know."

~ ~ ~

True to his word, Herb is waiting when she arrives. Her head is covered with a kerchief and large dark sunglasses hide her eyes. The baby bump is evident as she closes the car door. Herb gives her a tentative kiss, then places his hand on her belly. They enter the doctor's office. Karen signs in with the nurse and takes a seat next to her husband. Karen's face is still puffy. Her lips are chafed and cracked. The nurse tells Karen to follow her into the examination room.

The nurse consults with the doctor. "Doctor, your next patient waiting to see you is Mrs. Fishman."

The doctor senses that something isn't right. "What is the matter, nurse?"

"I haven't seen a woman this abused since Hedda Nussbaum."

"I see ... I remember that case only too well. It was back in 1987. Hedda Nussbaum and Joel Steinberg had custody of a little girl named Lisa. Together they made Lisa a punching bag. She died from a lack of love and was buried in The Gate of Heaven Cemetery. Joel Steinberg did 20 years and Hedda Nussbaum got a slap on the wrist, claiming she was a victim of domestic abuse."

"Correct, doctor. That was the gavel-to-gavel case that was televised. Poor Lisa fell through the cracks."

The doctor proceeds with the ultrasound. The baby is healthy, but he is concerned for her welfare. "I wish I could prescribe a pill for you to take that will alleviate the pain to your face, but I fear for the baby's safety. I want to see you in two weeks."

"Thank you, doctor. I will see you then."

Herb and Karen leave the office. The doctor jots down on her chart: notify child services after the child has been delivered.

Karen and Herb drive to Coney Island and have lunch at Nathan's. They take a stroll along the boardwalk as a stiff crisp wind blows in off the ocean. He tells her that for the time being he is staying with his mother, but he has to decide what to do with his father's business.

"Why did you hurt me, Herb? Wasn't I a good wife? I almost died, do you know that? Look at my face, go ahead look at it!"

"I messed up big time. I wasn't in my right frame of mind. But I promise, Karen, I have changed. If you'll just give me another chance, to make things right, I'll make it up to you."

The handle grip of the Glock rises above his waistband and Karen takes notice. "You have a gun, Herb? My God, what is all that about?"

"It is for my own protection."

"Who is out to get you, Herb, pray tell?"

"You know darn well, your crazy brother Sid and your father. They are out to get me. And I don't blame them because of what I did to you." He pulls out the gun and contemplates shooting himself. "I could end it all right now. You could be a rich widow and get on with your life."

"Erase that idea out of your head and put that gun away. I don't want my baby to be born without a father."

18

The newlywed couple was heading upstate on the New York Thruway. They were anticipating spending their honeymoon at Niagara Falls. They were running low on gas and could use a bite to eat, plus a rest stop. So they took the next exit and then followed a two-lane road for a couple of miles. Up ahead was a neon sign atop a roof that spelled out LUCKY'S Diner. The couple pulled into the gravel parking lot and noticed that there weren't a lot of vehicles. In the front window was a small sign posted: "FOR SALE inquire within." So the newlyweds found the nearest booth and sat down and read the menus.

The owner – an old timer named Harry Truman – yup, just like the president – asked the usual questions. Where are you from? Where are you headed? Then the husband asked Harry why he was selling the place. To which Harry replied, I just can't do it any longer. The long hours spent day-after-day ... well, I'm not getting any younger. So before they carry me out in a box, I'll hang up my apron and turn off the lights.

The wife inquires what he was asking for the diner. Harry sat down next to them, pulled a paper napkin from the holder, then took the pencil that was perched behind his ear and wrote down the asking price. Well, the number was attractive to the newlyweds, so they told Harry, "If after the honeymoon it's still up for sale we might be interested."

"Sure," said Harry. "I got a feelin' you two love birds will be back."

So here it is more than 50 years later and LUCKY'S is now LUC Y'S. The newlyweds Butch and Lucy bought old Harry out and soon thereafter Harry passed away. He was a veteran of WWII, saw action with old blood-and-guts General George Patton. Harry was a gunner's mate on a tank at the Battle of the Bulge. Harry had no next of kin, just a handful of friends, but Butch and Lucy made it a point to close the diner and attend Harry's funeral.

Now the flag that drapes a veterans casket is presented to a family member of the surviving spouse. Since Harry was a bachelor throughout his life, Butch and Lucy requested his flag. The flag found a proper resting place to be displayed in the diner, right next to Harry's apron.

About ten years ago, Butch was having trouble with his breathing. He thought nothing of it, figuring that the cigarettes were to blame. Oh Lord, how he tried to quit, but it was a hard habit to beat. He fought the good fight, taking the radiation and chemo treatments, but like anyone who has cancer the big C finds a way to take you out. Soon after Butch passed away, the letter K in LUCKY'S went out and the diner became better known as LUCY 'S.

The parking lot is filled with long-haul tractor-trailers from states far away. Montana, Utah, Wyoming, Arizona, Colorado, Minnesota, to name a few. The truck drivers keep their big rigs running while they eat and use the restrooms. The radio station is playing "Take It Easy" by the Eagles.

Sheriff Jasper Fast is on his second cup of coffee just after polishing off the breakfast special of a stack of blueberry pancakes, scrambled eggs, and whole wheat toast. He has the local newspaper spread out on the table of the booth when Brody Pence slides in across from him. Jasper is in his sheriff uniform and Brody is dressed in plain clothes.

"Morning, Jasper," Brody said.

"Morning, Brody. Will you look at what that knucklehead of a mayor in New York City is doing?" He points to the article in the newspaper. NYC looks to barriers to protect pedestrians. "To quote the pompous ass that just gave himself a 15% raise, no less. Listen to this, Brody. 'People have to be able to get around, but they have to be safe at the same time.' A lot of good that will do, Brody. Here it is shortly after the bombing at Macy's. The city is spending 50-million bucks to install 1,500 metal barriers and bollards so a car or truck can't mow down folks on the sidewalks."

Brody tells the waitress he'll have a cup of coffee, fried eggs over easy, sausage, and rye toast. "Hell, Jasper, why not hand everybody a gun to protect themselves. That way a terrorist or a lone wolf would think twice about plotting an attack in the City."

Jasper smiles at him. "Brody, I like the way you think. Yup, it would make our jobs a whole lot easier, for sure." Jasper takes a sip of his coffee. "There's another thing that sticks in my craw."

"What's that?" asks Brody as he seasons the eggs with the salt and pepper shakers.

"Legalizing pot. Do you know the once-removed Jesuit priest hippie flower-power transcendentalist governor of California, Jerry Brown, has proclaimed that getting high on cannabis is no longer a crime? It will bring in an estimated 5-billion for the state in taxes."

"You can bet that he's getting a kickback from the pot growers."

"Absolutely. Brody, you see it, I see it, but who in the Golden State will? The haze of smoke that will cover

San Francisco will be thicker than the fog comin' in off the bay."

One true giveaway no matter if you are playing poker trying to steal a base or a kiss our body language shows a *tell* what you are about to do. Every recruit who enters the police academy is drilled by their instructors who push them to their limit, be it physical training or mental toughness. The more in tune you are to your emotions the better you'll be after you pin on the badge.

The sheriff and the trooper share a unique talent, the ability to focus on where they are. They pay particular attention to the nearest exit and of who possibly could be in possession of a weapon or high on drugs. Their eyes dart back and forth as they talk like two sharks on the alert for predators.

"We are seeing an uptick in OD'S, Jasper. Especially the kids in high school. The government has to step up and supply us with Narcam that will save lives. Now if we receive a 911 call if it is an OD all we can do is wait for the EMS to arrive."

"Our hands are tied, Brody. Congress would rather spend time and money investigating Trump and his Russian connections. Who the hell cares, not me? Crack down on the drug dealers who are killing our kids, day-in day-out."

The waitress totals up the checks. Brody treats Jasper, paying for his breakfast. "Next time, it's on me," says Jasper.

As they are about to leave, a Mercedes Benz pulls into the parking lot. Behind the wheel is Fletcher; riding shotgun is Sid. The sheriff and the trooper take a quick glance as they walk pass the car. Fletcher and Sid wait until they drive off before exiting the car.

Sid makes a snide remark: "Smoky and the sheriff are in hot pursuit of the Bandit."

"Head for the hills," Fletcher replies.

They enter the diner and Lucy shows them to a booth in the rear. She hands them the laminated menus. "Take your time, but if you want the breakfast special order it soon or else the price goes up half a buck."

She turns over the coffee cups asks them if they want regular or decaf. Sid opts for decaf; Fletcher takes the regular. Sid pours the sugar shaker into the cup; Fletcher drinks his black.

"How much further to the casino?" Sid asks Fletcher.

"Not much further down the road. If the doctor's prescription is filled, then the Indian's will be back for more."

19

New York, the city that never sleeps and the streets are never deserted. The buses, subways, and taxis pick up and deliver their passengers to all of the boroughs. The Staten Island Ferry shuttles the riders to lower Manhattan where bankers, lawyers, and stock brokers conduct business with their clients. At One Police Plaza located at Chambers Street, the mayor and the police commissioner are embroiled in a rather intense conversation.

"The investigation of the Macy's bombing is taking too long to solve," the mayor shouted.

"We have the best forensic experts working around the clock. If you think you can do a better job, then be my guest," the exasperated PC replied.

"I expect a full report on my desk by the end of the week, or else I will find someone more competent to take your place."

"Go right ahead, Mayor. You've been nothing but a pain in my ass and for that matter every member of the NYPD. You think nothing about giving yourself a raise, but when it comes to the cops, not a penny more. You hold a press conference and tout how you have kept the city's budget in check by scaling back overtime. You have also shut down vital auxiliary command posts in high crime neighborhoods. And you side with Black Lives Matter. You never had our backs and yet we protect you and your family 24/7."

The Mayor has heard enough. "Don't think for a moment that your brother Mickey will save your job, Danny. The Como's are thick as thieves."

"Well, we are close, everybody knows that, Bill. But you are truly a piece of work using your mother's name Burattino instead of your father's. All for what, Bill, just to get the minority votes? You sold your soul to the devil and he will come a calling just as sure as a blizzard will cripple the City before the year is up."

The Mayor leaves the PC'S office. He might as well have been in high school, being chastised by the principal for being a truant, skipping out on class.

The PC takes the elevator to the basement where the NYPD command center is located. Ever since 9/11, when the Twin Towers came down, the NYPD moved its entire intelligence department to 1PP as a precaution in case of another terrorist attack.

The PC is updated on the Macy's bombing. After going through the surveillance footage of the day, a person of interest has been spotted that stands out in the crowd. The Santa suit that Ari Habbib wore went undetected at first glance, but after much scrutiny by the investigators they have come to the conclusion that indeed it fits the profile. But the enigma is that there is no footage of a Santa Claus entering the store. How did he manage to get past the tight security while the parade was underway?

Danny Como views the tapes as something catches his attention. "Roll that back to where Santa Claus places the candy cane." The female investigator complies. "There right there, freeze the frame." She dutifully obeys the PC. "See the bag, the Macy's bag with the candy cane. Watch as he takes it out. Okay, continue the footage. See now he doesn't leave the shopping bag at the scene, but rather he holds on to it tightly – why?"

"Maybe whatever was inside the bag was too valuable for him to leave behind," the female investigator replies.

"Exactly so, here's what we do. Roll back the tape to see who entered the store carrying the shopping bag just before Santa arrived to plant the explosives."

Within a few minutes, sure enough the image of Ari Habbib is seen disguised as a woman. "Do you think the bomber is a woman, police commissioner?" she asks.

"I wouldn't rule anything out just yet. But if it does turn out to be in fact a woman then ... we will be entering into new unchartered territory."

~ ~ ~

The Rockefeller Center is awaiting the latest arrival of what will be the tallest Christmas tree thus far. Last year a 95-foot Norway spruce was cut down in the Keystone State of Pennsylvania. This year not to be outdone by a rival state, a majestic tree was located upstate in New York. It was just by chance that a local radio station helicopter pilot who was monitoring the early morning rush hour traffic happened to glance down and see the top of the tree. He jotted down the exact location and passed it on to the local DJ. Before long, a representative of the Rockefeller Center rang the owner's doorbell.

Mr. and Mrs. Abernathy, both senior citizens, were taken aback. Their initial reaction was that it is a ruse for them to be chosen for such an auspicious occasion in New York City. The representative reassured them that his being there is strictly on the up and up, but still they had their doubts. So to prove to them that it is the real deal he calls 30 Rock and spoke with Matt Lauer. He then handed the phone to Viola as Vance listened in to the conversation. They are tickled pink and agreed to have their Norway spruce cut down.

"So where about are you located," Lauer asked the couple. "Well, we are in a little town in the Catskills. You probably never heard of it, Matt. The name of the town is Chirp." Matt Lauer chuckled along with the Abernathy's. "You got me there, for sure. You know I have been to many places. Maybe you might have seen my assignment segments where in the World Is Matt Lauer?"

"Oh yes, we are familiar with that. We enjoy them much so."

"Well, you have a nice day. And for being such a cute couple, the Today Show has invited you to be our guests when the tree is all aglow at Rockefeller Center."

"We will be there with bells on. Thank you ever so much."

On November 29th, the 100-foot Norway spruce is decorated with 50,000 lights and topped with a Swarovski star. There is a two-hour Rockefeller Christmas Spectacular Show featuring Tony Bennett, Billy Joel, Harry Connick Jr., Garth Brooks, and the Harlem Boys Choir. The skating rink is bathed in colors of red and green as the throngs of visitors gather to marvel at the event. Security is tight as the NYPD, SWAT, FBI, and members of the anti-terrorist group take up their positions.

Across the street from Rockefeller Center is St. Patrick's Cathedral. It is the residence of Cardinal Timothy M. Dolan, who oversees the Archdiocese of New York. The magnificent Cathedral has just been renovated inside and out. The previous three years scaffolding surrounded the perimeter. It was an extensive project repointing the limestone brick columns and touching up and restoring the frescos to their glory.

At the side entrance on 51st, Ari Habbib enters disguised as a priest. In his hand is a black missal that covertly conceals a bomb. A member of the SWAT team acknowledges him and allows him to proceed. The terrorist smiles to himself. So far, so good, he thinks. The evening Mass is being conducted as he moves about the Cathedral. He finds an empty pew next to one of the confessional booths. He waits until one of the penitent sinners departs, then he enters and draws the red velvet curtain to conceal himself. Through the darkened partition, he hears the priest say to him, "How can I help you?"

To which he replies, "What sins have you committed, father?"

The priest is taken aback "I beg your pardon. Are you here to confess your sins that are weighing heavy on your mind and in your soul?"

"I have many sins yet to commit. I just wanted to hear if you would divulge yours in the house of God."

"I tell my sins to the Cardinal and to no one else."

"I see father. Do you think I could speak with him?"

"No, that is not possible. He is resting in the Parish House, recovering from a bout of the flu."

"Well, in that case, father, since I can't help you and the Cardinal won't see me there is nothing else to say but I will see you in hell."

The priest slams shut the partition. Ari leaves behind the missal containing the bomb underneath the kneeler. He checks his watch, then quickly exits the Cathedral. He crosses the street, passing the crowds who are waiting for the mayor to light up the Rockefeller Christmas tree. Ali Habbib enters through the main entrance of Saks on 5TH Avenue. At the exact moment that the tree is to be lighted, he places a call from his burner phone to the bomb inside the confessional.

The bomb is packed with C4 explosives. The blast punches out a hole in the thick limestone wall and obliterates the confessional. Large chunks rain down on the pedestrians and the heavy traffic on 51st. The priest is ejected outward and onto the main aisle of the Cathedral. The statue of the Virgin Mary is blown to bits. Several of the 4,000 priceless stained-glass windows are shattered. The parishioners who are seated in the pews are impacted from the intense heat and debris. The votive glass candles are extinguished adjacent to the main altar as billowing clouds of white smoke fill the Cathedral. It is complete chaos as everyone scatters, leaving behind cellphones, purses, walkers, baby strollers, and Christmas gifts.

Ari Habbib enters the men's room in Saks, finds an empty stall, then removes the white clerical collar tosses it into the toilet bowl and flushes it away. He then removes the black jacket, turning it inside out, and now it is navy blue. He covers his head with a Rangers woolen cap and slips on a pair of Ray Bans to shield his eyes. He exits the stall, checks out his image in the mirror above the sink. And in his best impression of Jack Nicholson proclaims, "It's Showtime!"

20

Air France flight 503 touches down on the tarmac at JFK. Piles of snow dot the end on the runway, where the day before a Nor'easter blew in from the ocean causing blizzard conditions which cancelled flights up and down the Eastern Seaboard. Passing through US Customs is Shalimar Saddiq. She is dressed in jeans, a snug-fitting pullover sweater, and zip-up boots. On her shoulder is her carryon bag. She opens the bag, then takes out her passport and shows it to the customs agent.

He asks her the mundane question that is frequently asked: "What is your purpose for coming to the United States – business or travel?" To which she replies, "Travel." The French passport is stamped and she is allowed to pass through customs. Outside of the terminal, Shalimar hails a cab. She tells the driver her destination. With the amount of traffic on the Southern State Parkway and the Cross Island Parkway, it will take approximately three quarters of an hour to arrive at Ari Habbib's apartment.

It is a cold and blustery winter's day. The cars parked out on the streets are still covered with a mix of snow and ice. The cab pulls up in front of Ari's apartment. Shalimar pays for the ride, collects her bags, then carefully sets foot onto the slick and icy street. Joyce Owens, Ari's next-door neighbor, is busy scraping away the frost on her orange VW bug. She observes Shalimar as she enters Ari's apartment. He opens the door to let her in. He takes a fast peek outside to make sure she hasn't been followed from the airport. Once she is inside the apartment, Ari takes off her leather jacket and they waste no time getting reacquainted.

"It has been a long time," he said. "How have you been?"

"Very well, but France is quickly changing now that there is the newly elected President Macron. He is cracking down on the Muslims who have come from war-torn Syria. Macron has imposed a fine on women who wear the burkas. And he has outlawed Sharia. In retaliation there has been an uptick in bombings throughout France."

On the kitchen table is *The Daily News*. The headlines are in bold print. ST. PATS ATTACKED. Shalimar asks Ari the obvious question: "Is this your work, Ari?"

To which he replies, "That and the bombing at Macy's on Thanksgiving."

"My oh my, you have been a naughty little boy who needs to be taught a lesson."

She enters his bedroom, slips off the sweater, revealing a lacy pink bra. Ari unzips his pants and takes them off. Then he removes his boxer briefs. Shalimar unhooks the bra and slips it off. Ari pulls off her jeans and panties, then they get down to business.

Joyce turns off the car engine, then pushes the remote alarm attached to the ignition key, and returns to her apartment. The separation between Joyce and Ari's apartments is not soundproof, so she can hear their lovemaking through the wire-lathe sheetrock wall.

Shalimar shouts his name: "Ari!" Then she speaks in her native tongue, Farsi. Joyce is curious to hear more, so she places a glass tumbler on the wall to listen in. Ari replies to Shalimar, speaking to her in Hebrew. Joyce removes the glass away from the wall. "I knew there was something funny about that guy, but I couldn't put my finger on it."

Joyce zips up her snow parka, and then walks up to the Alley Pond Owners Corporation office at Springfield Boulevard. Mary Livingstone is single, middle-aged, and has short grey hair. She is petite, a smoker, and a closet lesbian. Joyce finds her at her desk. A strong gust of wind shuffles the papers in front of Mary as Joyce struggles to close the door. The gap at the bottom of the door can be felt on her ankles. Mary assumes that Joyce is there to pay the monthly maintenance fee. Mary dons her glasses and entertains a lesbian thought about Joyce.

"How can I help you?" she asks Joyce.

Joyce is tentative at first, but asks Mary, "What do you know about my next door neighbor?"

"Your next door neighbor, Joyce? The one upstairs or downstairs?" The Alley Pond apartments have only two floors, which share the same front entrance. Joyce and Ari live on the ground floor side-by-side.

"He is right next door to me on the first floor."

Mary jots down the address, then does a search in the Alley Pond apartment's records.

"He must be a subletter. Our records show that Allied International is the owner of the apartment."

"All well and good, but he must pay the rent to you, Mary."

"Not necessarily, Joyce. He pays it to Allied, who in turn sends it to us. Why are asking about him anyway? If you have a complaint, Joyce, then why not notify Allied International; not Alley Pond Owners Corporation."

Joyce is clearly miffed that Mary will not side with her concern. She leaves the office, walking back to her apartment where she bumps into Danny Montenez. Danny is tall and skinny, has black hair and a shaggy beard. He is dressed in a USPS uniform Danny is the mailman.

"Hi ya, Joyce. It sure is cold. You should be inside where it is cozy and warm."

"Not in my apartment, Danny. There's cracks in the windowsills and gaps under the front door. You would think that for the rent I pay, the place would be better taken care of by the owners. I wouldn't be surprised to find out that the boiler in the basement isn't functioning."

They are just about to part ways when she stops and asks Danny, "What do you know about my neighbor?"

"You mean the guy next door to you, left side or right?"

"The one on the left, Danny," she replied.

"Not much. He doesn't get mail other than circulars posted to the occupant."

"No bills, Danny?"

"Not a one, Joyce."

"Huh, it's like the guy don't exist. Thanks, Danny."

"Say, why all the questions about that guy anyway?"

"I can't say, Danny, but do me a favor if you can?"

"For you, Joyce, just name it."

"Find out about a company named Allied International. They own the apartment. Oh and by the way, Danny, I'm having a New Year's Eve party so if you're not doing anything, just come on by."

"You got it and thanks for the invite. I'll make sure to check out Allied once I get back to the Post Office."

Joyce returns to her apartment but before slipping the key into the front door, she rings Ari's bell. She could kick herself for being so forgetful, leaving her gloves and earmuffs on the coffee table. After a few minutes Ari opens the apartment door, then steps into the small entranceway to unlock the front door.

"Hi, sorry to bother you, but I'm hosting a New Year's Eve party in my apartment, so if you're not busy maybe you'd like to come on over." Shalimar is getting dressed and Joyce takes notice as she glances over Ari's shoulder.

"I don't think I will be here then, but thank you just the same." Ari starts to close the door.

"No problem. Silly me, my name is Joyce. And you are?"

He doesn't answer as the door is shut and locked.

21

Inside the Fishman's home a heated argument is ensuing between Herb and Brenda. Herb has just returned after going to his father's business. The locks have been replaced on the metal gates and the Shelly's neon sign has been removed.

"I had no choice," Brenda exclaims.

"What do you mean you had no choice?"

"Your father was heavy in debt, He never was a saver."

"But the store was always busy. Everyone in the neighborhood shopped there."

Brenda opens the liquor cabinet and takes out a bottle of Scotch, then pours herself a drink. "I think he tried to keep it a secret, Herb. He didn't want to disappoint you, his only child."

"So now what am I supposed to do? I don't have a job. Karen will be having a baby soon, then what?"

"Karen is pregnant? Mazel tov!" Brenda kisses Herb and gives him a warm hug. "Why haven't you told me?"

"I don't know … look, I need some money. Have you got a few bucks to get me by until I get back on my feet?"

Brenda slams the glass down on the granite-top kitchen island. "You maxed out my credit cards, now you want me to give you money? I'll tell you where you can go."

"Alright, ma. I get it. I screwed up big time, but I'm trying to get myself together. I have to if I am going to be a father."

Brenda picks up the phone and hands it to him. "Call the Stones. Maybe the doctor can find you a job."

"The Stones. No way, ma. My brother-in-law and me had a dustup a while back. The last thing I want to see is him."

"Listen Herb, I'll call Sylvia and tell her how excited I am to hear that Karen is expecting. Mothers can always find a way to smooth things over. You'll see, everything will work out okay."

It took a couple of phone calls back and forth before both families could come to terms. Herb was offered a job working for the doctor. It had been intended for Teddy to take Nick Morosco's job collecting kickbacks from Finn McCoole. Now it would be given to him instead.

The only stumbling block is how to keep the hot-tempered Sid from not killing Herb. Milton assumed that Sid and Herb would not cross paths in his home and that Karen was taken care of. For the time being, Karen would live at home until the baby was born. Then if Herb was good on the job, the doctor would buy them a house nearby.

The drugs that were smuggled inside the cheese wheels have been cut and placed into tiny plastic bags for distribution up in Harlem. The bags are sold on the streets as Fast Freddy. Out on the Island it is sold as Fish Fry. And in the five boroughs the street name is Powerball. The cash is coming in hand-over-fist. Now it is time to make the move up to the Catskills. If Stone can score an in at the Turning Stone Casino, he will make a killing.

But it is not as easy as he thinks. Malachi Eaglefeather is keeping a keen eye on the customers that walk through the doors. Ever since Fletcher was spotted on the security surveillance, he would be ready for a repeat appearance.

However the reason why Fletcher was there in the first place was just a trial run. Fletcher was checking out the casino for Stone to find out the type of customers who frequented the slots and the tables. Were they older who were down on their luck or was there money to be had? On the day that Fletcher was there it was more or less a mixed bag. So, Stone decided to roll the dice and go all in.

He would fill up his doctor bag with samples of the drugs and pay a visit to the casino. All the years that Stone has been a doctor has served him well. He has seen them all – the neurotics, the terminal cases, the psychos who hear voices in their heads, the patients who have a lower threshold when it comes to pain, the sadist who enjoy seeing other in pain, and the desperate who have asked him to terminate their life because the disease is slowing taking them little by little. So he would administer the drugs to help them with their misery.

He remembers how it was, watching his father succumb to dementia shortly after his mother's death from brain cancer. They would speak in whispers when he was just a child of their time in hell behind the barbed wire fences of Auschwitz. The Nazi guards would randomly select a man, take him out of the flea-infected and unheated wooden barracks in the dead of night and play sadistic games. The guards would place bets to determine which German shepherd was the fastest to bring down the prisoner. It really wasn't much of a game; it was a pack of angry dogs taking down a defenseless human being.

Night after night, Milton's parents witnessed the atrocities inflicted by the Nazi captors. One day all of the children were in the infirmary, totally segregated from the men and women. A female guard entered and told all of the children to form two lines, one for the girls, another for the boys. They did as they were told, all except for the doctor's parents. They hid in a closet that stored mops, brooms, and buckets. All of the children followed the female guard into the showers to get washed. Once the children were undressed, they stood waiting for the water to be turned on. But instead, chlorine gas poured from the showerheads. The children yelled and screamed as their tiny lungs filed with the toxic poison. The shower stall's walls were scraped by the children's fingernails, leaving behind evidence of what evil can do when one man can brainwash so many to carry out the Final Solution.

Now so many years later the memory of his parents still haunts him. Sometimes the doctor thought to himself, Aren't you in a roundabout way a Nazi? After all you are pushing dope that is deadly. The only difference is that you aren't wearing an SS uniform with a Nazi swastika armband.

22

The local Penny Saver had a notice advertising that a barn filled with farm equipment, hardware, car parts, and more was up for sale in the town of Woodstock. Like so many who live in small towns, there are several types of folk – those that collect and those that sell. Well, not really. There are the pickers (no, not nose pickers). Pickers go to swap meets, garage sales, antique shops, and flea markets.

Cody Pence is a picker whenever he saves up a couple of extra bucks in a rusty old coffee can that he keeps on the mantle above the fireplace. He'd tap into it and hit the road.

Cody filled up his pickup truck with a tankful of gas and drove to the location in Woodstock that posted the ad in the Penny Saver. The owner of the property was an old lady who had lived there for many years. Her husband had recently passed, so she needed to part ways with some of the items he had been collecting. Cody and the old lady went into the barn. She told him to take his time and if he saw anything that he might want to buy, just give her a holler. She'd be on the front porch in her rocking chair.

There were wooden boxes, oilcans, toys, tin canisters, old photos in scrapbooks. It was a hodgepodge to say the least. In the corner of the barn was a dusty and faded gray tarp that was covering an object that had two wheels. It caught Cody's eye so he pulled off the tarp to take a better look. To his surprise it was a Triumph motorcycle. The frame was painted silver and the gas tank was painted red.

The barn was dimly lit as the afternoon sun was behind a thick band of clouds. So Cody grabbed hold of the handlebars and rolled it out of the barn. He gave a whistle to the old lady who had just nodded off. She opened her eyes, then proceeded down the rickety wooden steps.

"How much do you want for this motorcycle?"

"Well now, let me see. Do you know if it has any gas in the tank?"

Cody removed the gas cap, then bent down to take a closer look. "It's bone dry"

"Oh dear, we're in a pickle barrel for sure. I'd hate to sell it to you not knowing if it runs. That's like selling you a cow that can't produce milk. Now what good is that?"

Cody walked around the bike. The tires are in decent shape, still inflated. All the original parts are intact, the only thing missing aside for the gas is the key to start it up. "Do you have the key for the motorcycle?"

"I'm sure it's around here somewhere, but exactly where I can't say."

"Do you mind if I take a look back inside the barn?"

"Sure thing. I'll be here a-waiting for you with my fingers crossed for good luck."

Cody searched high and low inside the barn, but no luck. It would be a waste of his money to buy the Triumph and not have the key to start it up. He was just about to give up the search when he spotted an old coffee can on a shelf next to the ladder of the hayloft. The contents of the can had pencil stubs, an old half of a pack of Camel cigarettes, a box of matches, and a ring of keys. Cody took the set of keys outside and as luck would have it one of them belonged to the Triumph.

The old lady's eyes were filled with delight. "Where in heaven's name do you find it?"

"It was in an old coffee can."

"Well, I'll be. In all the places to put it, my beloved kept it there."

Cody pulled out all of the money he had brought and showed it to her. "This is all I got. I've been saving it back home. Now you might not believe me, but it's true– in a rusty old coffee can."

The old lady did not hesitate; nope, not one itty bit, and then she placed her hands on Cody's and took the cash. Then without counting it, she peeled off a five-dollar bill and gave it to Cody. "That's for a tankful of gas."

Cody dropped the tailgate on the pickup, then found a loose plank propped up against the barn. Then he rolled the Triumph into the truck bed and secured it to the sides with rope. He had no idea just how valuable the motorcycle was.

A few days later there was an article in the local newspaper celebrating the anniversary of July 29th, 1966. Bob Dylan, who lived in Woodstock at the time, had been involved in a motorcycle accident. It was a Triumph Tiger 500cc. The article went on to state that it was a hoax concocted by Dylan so that he could get some peace and quiet and be with his family. Along with the article there was a photo of the motorcycle.

It was a dead ringer to the one that Cody bought from the old lady in Woodstock. Cody opened up a shop in Echo Lake. Cody's Cycle Shop is where he prominently displays the Triumph and the newspaper article. Soon word spread around that Dylan's bike had been found after all those years. Billy Joel and Bruce Springsteen, who own and ride motorcycles, visited the shop and had their pictures taken with the prized Triumph along with Cody.

Brody Pence is Cody's cousin. He grew up back in Jackson Heights, Queens. Brody followed in his family's footsteps and became a member of the law enforcement. He took the New York State Troopers test and passed. He was assigned to a troop out on Long Island at first, chasing after drivers speeding on the Long Island Expressway. Then Brody took the test for sergeant and again he passed. He was then assigned to K Troop in Upstate New York and was forced to relocate to be closer to the barracks.

Brody, who hadn't seen Cody in years, was looking for a place to stay when he happened to pass the cycle shop. He had no idea it belonged to Cody, and with his help Brody moved into a log cabin that overlooked Echo Lake.

"So what brings you up here, Brody?"

"I was transferred to be part of the undercover taskforce that is going to take down the drug dealers. Say, you have a nice shop Cody. I bet you come across a lot of customers wanting to buy a fancy Harley or an Indian. I'm new in town and like anyplace when somebody new moves in, the local yokels need to know all about them. Cody, if you spread the word that I work for you as a part time mechanic, I could keep my undercover role safe."

"Sure, no problem, no sweat, Brody. Hey, blood's thicker than water, right?" They bump their fists, then Brody takes off.

Cody places a call to the Two Timer's. Buster Coogan picks up the phone. "Hey, it's me, Cody. Say, is Finn around?"

"No, he's not. Did you try calling his cellphone?"

"I don't have the number. Anyway give him this message."

Coogan grabbed a piece of paper and a pen. "Okay, Cody, what's the message for Finn?"

"Tell him if he's going to move the product up to me, no sweat. I got good news. Now make sure he gets this."

"Sure thing. Do you want him to call you back?"

"Not at this number. Just in case he has my cellphone, have Finn text me."

"Will do, Cody. Bye," Coogan said.

23

Ever since the latest incident at St. Patrick's, the security in NYC has been on high alert. The mayor is taking the heat from the governor, who in turn has been pressured by President Trump to get the bastard or else he will find a way to have them FIRED! All of the NYPD have been working overtime and the tension is slowly beginning to show. Inside the 61st Precinct, Capt. Millwood is having a conniption. His phone is constantly ringing off the hook in regards to an uptick of drug related deaths.

Pickett and Dobbs have been looking for leads to solve the murders of Morosco, Fishman, and Mary Dunham, but so far not a clue.

Pickett dropped an envelope on his partner's desk.

"What's this?" Dobbs asked. "Open it go ahead Chuck and find out." Dobbs pulled from the envelope three tickets to Madison Square Garden for an upcoming Rangers game against the Islanders. He can't believe his eyes.

"Holy shit, Bruce, how did you score these?"

"I told you, I know a guy who knows a guy. Check out where the seats are, right behind the Rangers bench."

"No way Jose. Okay ... what's the catch? Tell me what do I owe you in return?"

"Just add it to the tab, Chuck."

Dobbs looked at the date of the game printed on the tickets: Dec 31st. "New Year's Eve, there's no way

Millwood will let me go. You saw Como and Burattino at their latest news conference declaring a state of war against whoever was responsible for the bombings at Macy's and St. Pat's."

"Look, we'll both go and see the Captain in his office, and maybe you could do a switcheroo with a plainclothes cop at the Garden."

"Well, if that's the case, then you're coming with me as backup."

"Yeah but I only got the three tickets for you and the kids."

"Then you better text your contact to find you an extra ticket."

Capt. Millwood wasn't in the best of moods to say the least, but he respects the detectives and they have the highest arrests in the stationhouse. So reluctantly he let them go to the game. But there is one caveat. "Come January 1st I better see your sorry asses here bright and early in the morning."

"You got it Captain and thanks a lot," replied Pickett.

On New Year's Eve, NYC is having one of the coldest December 31st ever recorded, +5 above zero but with the wind chill factor it might as well be -10. The crowd in Times Square had been arriving since 6 a.m. passing through metal detectors as specially trained canines patrol the streets and subway entrances, detecting any possible threats. If ever there was the potential to have a perfect storm for another terrorist strike, right here in front of millions around the world tuned in on their electronic devises, this would be the optimum moment.

~ ~ ~

Joyce Owens is busy hanging a Happy New Year's sign across her living room wall. On the kitchen table are an assortment of party hats, poppers, and whistles.

On the coat rack are plastic Hawaiian leis that she will give to the guests. The ice chest is filled with beer and soda. All she has to do is step into the shower, then figure out what to wear for the party.

Ari and Shalimar have plans also for New Year's Eve. They leave the apartment just as Joyce steps out of the shower. She wraps a towel around her wet body, then walks into the living room. Through the window Joyce observes Ari and Shalimar carrying duffle bags as they walk down the street to the bus stop.

"Damn if there was only a way for me to get into his apartment," she thinks to herself. She snapped her fingers. "I got it, yes."

Joyce throws on a pair of jeans slips into her bra pulls on a FDNY sweatshirt, then laces up the black boots. She made a call to the Alley Pond maintenance office and told Mary that she smelled a strong odor coming from Ari's apartment.

"Did you call the fire department?" Mary asked.

"No not yet," Joyce replied.

"I'll have the maintenance man, Doug, come on over with the keys to the apartment to check it out."

"Thanks, Mary," Joyce said, ending the call.

Doug arrived dressed in a brown uniform. He is to say the least a mite slow on the uptake. Joyce met him on the front stoop. "Are you the one who called about smelling gas?"

"Yes I did."

Doug digs the keys from the pocket in his jacket. He opened the outside door, then unlocked the door to Ari's apartment. Doug headed straight to the kitchen to check on the stove and the top burners, while Joyce made a beeline to the bedroom. She opened the closet to find the Santa suit along with a Fed Ex uniform and an airline stewardess uniform. She rifled through the dresser drawers just as Doug walked out of the kitchen.

"You sure you smelled gas coming from this apartment?"

Joyce stepped out from the bedroom.

He looked at her with suspicion. "Hey, what were you just doing in there, snooping around on your neighbors things?"

Joyce, quick as a fox, replied, "I just wanted to make sure there wasn't a gas space heater in the bedroom that could cause a potential fire."

Doug nodded his head. "That's good thinking. I would have just checked the kitchen and walked out."

"Thanks, Doug. Could you do me a favor? If you see the guy who has this apartment don't tell him about this."

"Well now I ..."

Joyce slips him a tip for his troubles and to keep it on the QT.

"You got it," he says. "My lips are sealed."

~ ~ ~

Shalimar and Ari take the bus to Bell Boulevard where they boarded the Long Island railroad train that will take them to Penn Station. Directly above the station is Madison Square Garden. They quickly made their way to the restrooms where they switched out of their clothes in exchange for MSG security uniforms. They zip up the duffle bags and made their way into the arena.

Pickett and Dobbs, along with his kids in tow, have arrived at the main entrance. They get their tickets scanned and Pickett flashed his detective's badge that granted him admission. Then Dobbs and the kids found their seats. Bobby is wearing a Rangers jersey and Mindy is all decked out in her favorite color pink. She is totally bored while she checked her cellphone.

Chuck pointed out the large banners hanging high above the Garden. "Wow, look at that, Mindy. Billy Joel and Elton John have played the most shows at the Garden. Maybe we could get tickets to see them?"

"Dad they're old school. Who listens to them anyway?"

"I do, Mindy," Bobby chimed in.

"Whatever," Mindy replied.

Dressed in the uniforms, Ari and Shalimar manage to elude security. Ari located the Zamboni machine, while Shalimar kept a keen eye out for anyone who would question their being there. Ari went straight to work. He unzipped one of the duffel bags and removed a battery attached to a detonator and C4 explosives. He set the timer so that the bomb will explode when the Zamboni is on the ice between the 1st and 2nd period of the hockey game. Then they proceed to the concession area, find an unoccupied table, and prepare for the inevitable.

The hockey game has three twenty-minute periods and two ten-minute intermissions. The first period is well played; the Islanders scored the first goal. Seated in the penalty box for the Rangers was Rick Nash. That allowed John Taveres to score by beating the goalie Henrik Lundqvist. But Nash got even just seconds before the horn sounded on a breakaway that goalie Jaroslav Halak could not stop.

As Nash was being interviewed by Pierre McGuire, the Jumbotron captured Dobbs and the kids. Bobby's eyes lit up with glee. "Hey, look, Mindy. We're on the big screen."

Mindy is too busy texting to take her eyes off her cellphone.

Dobbs asked the kids if they wanted something to eat or drink. Bobby wanted a hot dog and soda; Mindy asked for a bottle of water. Dobbs made his way up to the concession area where he bumped into Pickett. Seated nearby are Ari and Shalimar.

"Hey, Bruce, thanks again for the seats. They're great. What can I get you to eat?"

"I could sure go for a cold beer and some fries."

"You got it, partner."

While they stand on line waiting to be served, the Zamboni machine is being maneuvered on the ice. The blades shave off any uneven spots, then the machine coats the ice rink with water. As the driver steered the Zamboni closer to the Rangers bench, Ari checked his wristwatch. He turned to look at Shalimar, then counted down backwards 10-1.

Then the explosion took place.

The Zamboni is blown into pieces. The driver was catapulted into the Islanders bench minus his left leg. The wheels were propelled into the seats where a woman was decapitated and an usher was knocked down in the aisle. The razor sharp blades were ejected. Had it not been for the thick Plexiglas partition, Bobby and Mindy would have been seriously injured. The engine of the Zamboni took most of the impact from the bomb and yet it was still functioning as the remains went around in circles.

Dobbs and Pickett instinctually react to the carnage in the Garden. While everyone was running for the exits, Shalimar and Ari remained in their seats as if nothing happened. The two detectives made a mad dash to where Bobby and Mindy are. They push aside the fans that are crowding the aisle, moving in the opposite direction. Mindy is crying, holding tight to Bobby.

"Are you okay?" Dobbs asked his kids.

"We're okay, dad. What just happened?" his daughter wanted to know.

Pickett spotted the badly injured Zamboni driver and he assisted him by applying his belt as a tourniquet to the severed limb. The distinct smell of explosives filled the arena. The black smoke from the Zamboni's engine covered the ice rink.

The pair of terrorists blended into the crowd as they proceeded to the nearest exit. They ditched the duffel bags into a trash bin.

The escalators are not functioning so the stairwells are jam-packed.

Pickett and Dobbs reunite. Bruce patted Bobby's head, then lightly squeezed Mindy's hand. They know it will take a while to empty the arena, so they did their best by shielding the deadly scene from the kids, but too little avail. There is so much damage from the Zamboni being blown to bits. The broad brush, the blade bolts, along with the down pressure spring became shrapnel that gravely impacted the innocent bystanders. They cannot comprehend what just went down.

"What's the capacity of the Garden, Bruce?"

"18,000, more or less, I'd guess."

"I was just thinking how many suspects there could be to have pulled this off."

"My money is on the spooks that did Macy's and St. Pat's."

"Same here, partner. We got our work cut out for us, for sure."

24

Fletcher and Sid parked the car inside the Turning Stone garage, then proceeded into the casino. It is early in the afternoon and the casino's card tables are closed until after 6 p.m. So they decided to play the craps table and chance their luck.

Malachi is inside the teller's cage when he noticed them. He placed a call to the sheriff. "Hey, Jasper, that black guy is here in the casino."

"Thanks, Malachi. Is he alone?"

"No, there's a white guy with him that I haven't seen before."

"Make sure they don't leave. I'm on my way."

Jasper Fast straps on his holster, checked the clip in his gun, and grabbed the keys to his truck as he left the sheriff's office. It didn't take but a few minutes before he pulled into the Turning Stone Casino grounds. The parking attendant directed him to a spot designated for VIP visitors. Jasper exited the truck, and then entered into the casino where Malachi waited to greet him. The Indian pointed to the craps table where Fletcher and Sid were placing their bets.

"See the black guy, Jasper? That's who I saw driving the car that night."

"I saw both of them just the other day over at Lucy's diner."

They approached them. Sid has the dice in his hands and is chewing on a wad of gum. Fletcher is chatting up the cute little waitress as he removed two glasses of liquor from her tray. Fletcher turned around to face Malachi and Jasper standing in front of him.

"Do you remember me?" Malachi asked him.

Fletcher, who was wearing fancy gold colored sunglasses, lowered them to the tip of his nose. "Can't say that I do" he replied.

"Try again. A few weeks ago you were driving a Mercedes Benz. You had two guys in the backseat. You were parked outside the main entrance of the casino. I came along and gave you directions back to the Interstate."

Fletcher removed the sunglasses. "Oh shoot, now I remember that was you. Hey, brother, what can I say?"

To which Jasper stepped up and asked him point blank, "Did you kill Nick Morosco?"

Sid heard what the sheriff had just said. He got all up into Jasper's face. "You can't ask him any questions. This here is private property we're on."

Jasper pokes Sid in his chest. "Why don't you keep your trap shut or I'll find something to accuse you of. And for your information I was requested by the casino to investigate a murder that took place in my jurisdiction." He then turned back to Fletcher. "I'll ask you again, did you kill Nick Morosco?"

"I don't know who that is."

Now it is Malachi's turn to ask the question. "We have you on tape entering and leaving here driving a Cadillac Escalade."

"So can't a black man drive a fancy SUV without being accused of a crime?" Fletcher downed the drink he is clearly getting agitated.

"The SUV was leased to Nick Morosco, whose body was found not far from here in the woods close to Peekamoose Mountain. So you either killed him or you were an accomplice to his sudden death. What is it?" Jasper asked him.

"Am I under arrest?" Fletcher defiantly asked.

Before Jasper can respond, Sid all cocky told him, "You need a warrant to lock him up. Have you got one, sheriff?"

"No, I do not, punk, but when I do I'll make damn sure to have one to haul your sorry ass in as well."

"Am I free to go," Fletcher asked.

"For now, but don't think that this matter is over, not by a long shot."

Fletcher and Sid continued to place their bets at the craps table while Malachi and Jasper walk away. "So now what, sheriff?" Malachi asked him.

"How do the payouts work here at the casino? You know, does the gambler have to show proof of identity when they cash in their chips?"

"No, they do not. Unlike any other casino that is regulated by the government, where a 1099 tax form has to be filled out before they can collect their winnings."

"I see. Boy, I'd sure like to know who that smartass was with the black guy. Are you certain, Malachi, that he wasn't in the car that night with Morosco?"

"I can't say for sure, sheriff. Like I said, the other guy in the backseat was in the shadows. So maybe it was him. But he was older, this much I know."

25

Later that night inside the Two Timer's, Buster Coogan is putting away the New Year's Eve decorations from the party the night before. Finn McCoole is going over the receipts when he receives a text message on his cellphone. The package is ready to be picked up. The Irishman has been anticipating the latest delivery of heroin. It is being shipped in boxes of imported chocolate from Switzerland and has arrived dockside in Red Hook. He has a tough decision to make, alert the doctor where he will get a small percentage or keep it for himself.

Finn has Cody Pence to distribute the merchandise upstate and Stone knows nothing about this. He could pick up the latest delivery and bring it back to the bar. But knowing how shrewdly the doctor conducts business, he probably has spies checking out his every move. So just to be sure he called Stone at his home.

The conversation is short and brief. Then Finn asked the doctor, "Are you busy tonight?"

"As a matter of fact, I was about to make a trip up to Harlem. Why, what's up?"

Finn hesitated before he answered. "No, nothing. I just thought you were coming to the bar to pick up what's due for you."

"Not tonight, Finn. Herb will be around sometime tomorrow to collect. I don't know where the hell Sid and Fletcher are. They must be stuck in traffic coming back from the Indian casino. If they aren't here in ten minutes, then I'll have to take Herb with me up to Harlem."

Finn McCoole is curious to know where Stone is headed. "Say, Doc, where exactly do you go up in Harlem? You know you have to be careful in that neighborhood. They sure don't put out the welcome mats for us white folk."

"I'm sure that I'll be just fine. 147th and Lex is as safe as midtown and 5th Avenue."

"Okay then. Well, have yourself a good night."

Coogan wiped down the bar, then pushed a cardboard box across the wooden floor. "I was just thinking when we were just lads back in Belfast."

"Ah yes, those were the days, me bucko. Pour me a pint of Guinness and you as well."

Finn looked down at the box. It is filled with assorted Halloween masks. They finished their drinks, then Finn told Coogan to close up the bar.

"But it's still early. We'll lose a lot of money." There are just a handful of customers.

"Just do as I say." Finn picked up the cardboard box and tucked it under his arm. "I'll meet you outside by the car."

The Irish bartender gave the barflies the bad news. They grumbled to themselves as they down their drinks. Coogan shuts off the lights and locks the bars door. He slips in behind the steering wheel. Finn is seated next to him.

"Okay, where are we going that can't wait?"

"We're going to pay the doctor a visit."

"He lives on Surf Avenue, am I correct, Finn?"

"Yeah, but we're going uptown to Harlem."

Coogan looked at Finn with a serious expression on his face. "You can't be serious, Finn."

"That I am. After tonight the drugs in the city will be controlled not by a Jew but by a Mick."

Coogan has a shiteating grin on his face as he turned the key to start up the car. He checked the mirrors, put the car in gear, and pulled away from the curb.

~ ~ ~

Herb found a parking spot a few doors down from Belinda's brownstone. Stone stepped out and told Herb that he will be back shortly. Stone grabbed the black satchel from the back seat as a few drops of rain pelted the street. He pulled the collar up on his jacket, and then proceeded up the street.

Coogan steered the black Chevy Impala slowly down the street, then Finn told him to pull up next to the fire hydrant. Finn pulled out a Barack Obama Halloween mask from the cardboard box and slipped the hood of the sweatshirt over his head. He pulled on a pair of black gloves, gripped the gun tightly, and zipped up the jacket before exiting the car. He waited for the traffic in the street to pass, then followed Stone up the brownstone steps.

Finn pointed the gun at Stone's back and squeezed the trigger two times. Stone's knees buckled as he attempted to grab hold of the wrought iron railing. He dropped the black satchel. It bounced down the steps, landing at the foot of McCoole. McCoole quickly snatched the bag and made a hasty dash back across the street. Coogan pushed open the passenger door, then hit the gas for a fast getaway.

"Is he dead?" Coogan asked him.

"I don't know. I was pretty close enough to take him out, but then I froze. Get going, Coogan. Move it, move it!"

Herb rushed to Stone who was gasping for breath. Belinda opened the front door. She was dressed in a sheer nightgown as she bent down to caress the head of

Stone in her lap. Blood trickled down the side of his mouth.

"Call 911," Herb told her. Belinda rushed back inside to call for an ambulance. "Stay with me, Milt. Help is on the way. Don't you dare die on me you hear? I have you, hold on." The doctor was losing consciousness as his eyes dilated. He continued to gasp as the light rain intensified. Belinda threw on a silk robe and was standing at the top of the stairs when the ambulance arrived.

The EMT'S strapped the doctor to the stretcher and placed him in the back of the ambulance.

"What hospital are you taking him to?" Herb asked them.

The black female paramedic replied, "Bronx Lebanon, which is the closest." She hooked up an IV, then took the doctor's vital signs. "Did you see what happened?" she asked.

"No, I was parked down the street. It all happened so fast."

"Are you related to him?"

"Yes, he is my father-in-law. He is a doctor."

The back doors are closed, the lights and sirens activated, and the ambulance drove away. Herb followed in his car. He was sweating profusely. What is he going to say to the family? How will Sid react? Surely he will blame him for his father being shot. The ambulance arrived at the emergency entrance of the hospital. The paramedics moved swiftly, transferring Stone to a staff of nurses and interns. Herb parked the car in the hospital parking lot, then walked into the main entrance where he was directed by a receptionist to take the elevator to the third floor.

The hospital is filled with patients waiting to be treated for all sorts of diseases, injuries, intoxication, and overdoses. Herb located Stone in the hall, lying in a hospital bed. His shirt and jacket are covered in his blood. Herb asked one of the nurses when he will be operated on. She told him as soon as there is an available surgeon. Herb had to make the phone call to notify the family what happened. He dreaded that but reluctantly he did.

Sylvia picked up the phone. "Milt has been in an accident."

She did not comprehend what Herb was talking about. "Is he all right?" Sylvia asked him.

"I am with him in Bronx Lebanon up in Harlem."

"Harlem? What the hell is he doing up there? For God's sake, Herb, you aren't making any sense."

He tried to make the call short as he told her the doctor is attending to him. "I have to go, Sylvia. Tell Karen that I love her."

No sooner had she put the phone down when Sid and Fletcher arrived home. Sylvia is clearly upset. "Don't take off your jacket. Herb just called. Your father has been in some sort of an accident."

"Where, ma? Is he all right?"

She grabbed for her purse, donned her coat and scarf, then shouted to Karen and Teddy who are in the basement playing video games. "Stop what you're doing. Daddy is hurt and we have to go see him."

As Fletcher drove, Sid was getting himself all worked up. "What the hell was Herb doing with dad? If he had something to do with this, I'll kill him. I swear to God, I will!"

Karen defended her husband. "Herbie wouldn't do that, Sid. Daddy gave him a job when nobody else would. I'm sure that as soon as we get to the hospital we'll find out what happened."

Herb is pacing the floor in the visitors lounge when the family arrived. Karen hugged Herb; he gave her a kiss. Sid had his hands clenched into fists. "So what the hell happened to my old man?"

"I took him up to Harlem. He waited for you and Fletcher to arrive. But when you didn't show up, I took my car up to 147th and Lex. He got out of the car, told me to wait. Then I heard two shots, bang bang."

"Shots? Gun shots?" Sylvia shouted out loud.

"Yes, it happened so fast."

Sid had heard enough that he wanted to punch Herb, but Fletcher held him back.

"Who would want to kill Poppa?" Teddy wanted to know.

"That is a good question, kid," replied Fletcher.

Sid was not done with Herb. "This is your fault, you gutless piece of shit."

Herb had heard enough from him. "Bullshit. Where were you? I was the one who drove him up to Harlem. I was the one who made sure that an ambulance was called ASAP. If not for me, he would have died right there on the brownstone steps."

Fletcher knew only too well where Stone was shot – at Belinda Bellows a/k/a Sweet Magnolia's residence. The door to the visitors lounge opened and in stepped Dr. Tempest Hamilton. She is a Jamaican. Tall and slender, her hair is done up in short dreadlocks. Her eyes are crystal green. She is dressed in green scrubs and wearing a white pair of Crocs shoes. A stethoscope is draped around her neck. She talks with a pronounced West Indian accent.

"I am Doctor Hamilton. I will be the attending surgeon for Mr. Stone."

"He is also a doctor. My husband is a good man. Can you tell us how he is?"

"He is in very serious condition. The bullets entered his back. He has a collapsed right lung and the other injury is very close to his spine. I have to tell you that it does not look good. But I can assure you he has the best team of doctors and nurses that will be assisting me in the operation."

Karen asked her, "Do you know how long the procedure will take?"

"It is too early to tell. Why don't you go home and get some rest. I will call you as soon as he is out of the OR." The doctor departed.

Words were bantered about as if they were playing a game of badminton. "Whoever did this, I swear to God I'll get them and when I do they are dead" Sid exclaimed as he punched the wall with his fist.

Teddy walked over to his brother. "What we have to do is figure out who wanted him dead. If they find out the he survived the hit maybe, just maybe, they might come here to complete the rubout."

"Oh my God, Teddy, what are you saying?" Sylvia replied as she opened her purse looking for the packet of tissues. Her hands trembled as she sat next to Karen.

"Why don't you all go home and I'll stay. Sid, Fletcher, and you too, Herb, go about my father's business as usual. Keep your ears open and your eyes peeled. Somebody who is close to Poppa had something to do with this, I am certain," Teddy told them.

"You're going to watch over Pop? That isn't going to happen. I stay and you go home."

Karen sided with her younger brother. "No, Sid. Teddy's right, we should all go home. You can never tell, maybe whoever shot Daddy has their eyes watching the house, waiting for an opportunity to finish the job."

"All this talk, my God. My husband is a doctor, for Pete's sake. You talk as if he is a mobster. He takes care of sick people, not hoodlums. You think I wouldn't know if he was up to no good? Aw Milton, what were you doing up here in the middle of the night?"

The family and Fletcher leave while Teddy stayed behind. The late news was televised in the visitor's lounge informing the viewers about Dr. Milton Stone being shot in Harlem.

Inside Finn McCoole's apartment he watched the news on his television set. The news reporter mentioned that Stone is still alive and had been taken to Bronx Lebanon Hospital. McCoole got Declan McDermit up from his bed, turning on the bedroom light. "C'mon, we got a job to do."

The operation is over. Doctor Hamilton conveyed the good news to Teddy while she pulled off the latex gloves. "We were unable to remove one of the bullets closest to the spine. It has to remain in his back or else he could be paralyzed from the waist down. He will have to use a wheelchair to get around for the time being."

"Thank you, doctor. Can I see him?"

"Yes, but not for long. He is heavily sedated. Follow me and I'll show you to his room."

Teddy entered the room. His father was hooked up to an IV. There was a needle in his arm covered with a bandage. Teddy pulled up a chair and sat beside him. "I love you, Poppa," he said as he took his father's hand.

The door to the room opened and in stepped Belinda Bellows. She is dressed in a full-length silver fox coat, diamond rings on her fingers, and three strands of pearls around her slender neck. Her wrists and arms are covered with large bangle bracelets and flashy golden hoops hang down from her ears. She is holding a bouquet of fresh roses.

"You must be Teddy. Your father has told me all about how proud he is of you."

Teddy can smell her sweet lavender-scented perfume as she bent over to give Stone a kiss. The coat opened and her low cut dress revealed her ample cleavage for Teddy to gaze at. "Who are you anyway?"

"I'm a good friend of your father, Teddy. He was at my apartment when he was shot."

"Your apartment for what reason. I don't ... I don't understand. Are you a patient of his?"

She smiled, flashing her pearly white teeth. "In a roundabout way, you can say that. Your father has been very good to me. He is the only doctor I would allow to make house calls. And I in turn would accommodate him by paying him off in trade."

"In trade, Miss? With what?" he asked.

Belinda Bellows turned on the charm as she placed her hand on his thigh, then slowly moved her fingers ever so closer to his crotch. Teddy's face turned beet red as he began to get aroused. He pushed her hand away, then walked over to the window where he spotted Finn McCoole and Declan McDermit down in the street. Teddy ran over to his father's bed. He sensed that they are out to harm his father.

"You have to help me move his bed."

"What for?" she wanted to know.

"Look, we don't have much time. There's two men on their way to harm him. We have to move him to another room."

Together they pushed and pulled the hospital bed out into the hall. At the nurses station, Dr. Hamilton took notice.

"What are you doing?" she asked.

"We need to find another room for my father. Two men are on their way to finish him off. Will you help us?"

Hamilton had to make a quick decision. If they move the doctor to another room it will be only a matter of time before they find out where he is. "Take him down the hall and into my office. He'll be safe in there and I'll lock the door as a precaution."

No sooner have they moved him into the office than Finn and Declan stepped out of the elevator. They walked into Stone's room with their guns drawn, but to their surprise it is empty. They put away their hardware, then approached the nurses station.

"Can I help you gentleman?" Doctor Hamilton asked.

"Yeah, we're looking for Dr. Stone. He isn't in his room. Do you know where we can find him?" Finn asked her.

"Yeah, we'd love to see him to cheer him up," Declan added.

"I see. Are you members of the family?"

"Nah, just old friends. We go way back. We just wanted to pay our respects for old time sake."

"Well, Doctor Stone has been released so I guess right about now he is on his way back home. He has a long road to a full recovery, so if I were you two I'd wait a while before paying him a visit."

They push the button for the elevator, then leave. Hamilton waited until she saw them walking back to the parking garage before she unlocked her office. "The coast is clear they just left." Together they moved Stone back into his room.

"Thank you for helping me to safe guard my father from serious harm."

Dr. Hamilton looked at Belinda. "Well, I know for a fact that you aren't a member of the Stone family, unless you are the black sheep who wishes to remain anonymous."

"No, doctor. I'm Belinda Bellows, but a lot of my clientele know me better as Sweet Magnolia."

"I see ... so were you the focal point why my patient is lying here in this hospital bed?"

Belinda lowered her head in shame. "Sorry to admit it, but that is true. I am the cause for his tragic situation."

"I don't really care what your occupation is. I can surely guess from the clothes and the bling that you must charge a pretty penny. But come on now, an old Jewish doctor as one of your johns? "

"Hey, a girl's gotta do what a girl's gotta do. And besides he is one hell of a lover."

Teddy has heard just about enough of what she is saying about his father. "That's not true. He adores my mother. He is loyal as the day is long."

The hooker batted her long false eyelashes, blew a kiss to Stone as she exited the room.

"You are a brave young man. It took a lot of courage taking into your own hands what had to be done on a moment's notice. You made a split decision to move your father out of harm's way."

"And I, in turn, doctor want to thank you for saving my father's life. I only hope that perhaps one day I can repay you my debt of gratitude."

26

Ari and Shalimar have eluded the dragnet thus far, but it will be only a matter of time before they are captured. Shalimar donned the airline stewardess uniform that was hanging in Ari's closest and made a fast getaway. Ari called for a cab to pick her up outside the apartment. Joyce is next door getting ready to pull a shift at the firehouse. She zipped up her large gym bag, then stepped outside. The cab pulled up to take Shalimar to the airport. Ari kissed her goodbye and helped her with the luggage.

"I didn't know that your girlfriend was a stewardess," Joyce said to Ari.

"Heck no, she's not my girlfriend. We're old friends, nothing more than that." He noticed the gym bag in her hand. "Are you going to the gym to work out?"

"No, I'm off to work." Joyce started to walk away.

"Really, so like what do you do?"

Joyce doesn't know what to tell him at first and then she replied, "I'm a firefighter." Being the savvy New Yorker she is Joyce asked him, "How about you? Where do you work?"

"I'm a telemarketer, so I have the luxury of working from home."

Joyce pushed the remote car alarm on her VW bug, then waved goodbye. When she arrived at the firehouse in Red Hook, Brooklyn, she stored her gear in the locker, and then checked in with the fire captain.

Captain Hector Dante is a Puerto Rican, a rugged-looking guy with streaks of gray in his hair and beard.

"Hi Captain, I'm just checking in."

"Firefighter Owens, today is your lucky day." Dante handed her a plastic cup. "You are going to be tested for drugs, so the department needs a sample of your urine. Are you okay with that, Firefighter Owens?"

"Sure, no sweat, Captain. Whatever you say."

"Here at the Happy Hookers engine 279, ladder 131, we take our jobs seriously. Last year a fellow smoke-eater was selling Vicodin and Xanax right outside the house. The balls of that bastard. There is a daycare center, the Choo Choo Train, three blocks from here. Thanks to him the captain got transferred. So I don't want anyone in my house taking that dirt bag's place. "

"I read you loud and clear, Captain. I am in full cooperation with the regulations of the NYFD."

"You're still a probie, so everything you say and do will be scrutinized. The NYFD plants agents of the IAB from time to time to keep tabs on the men and women."

Joyce took the plastic cup and went into the women's bathroom and peed into it. She printed her name with a black Sharpie on the lid and returned it to the captain.

"Say, Captain, I know this is going to sound crazy but I need to tell someone I can confide in."

"Fire away. What's on your mind?"

Joyce recounted everything she had observed about Ari and Shalimar.

"From what you divulged to me I think you should get in touch with the NYPD, ASAP."

"Thanks Captain. I just wanted to pass it on to you. Me being a probie, I didn't want to overstep the chain of command."

"Go ahead, Owens. Make the call to the cops."

Joyce called Maureen Flynn on her cellphone. Maureen is in bed at Detective Pickett's apartment. She has just finished up a double shift at Coney Island Hospital. Maureen reached over Bruce to answer the call.

"Hey, Maureen. Am I catching you at a bad time?" Bruce is aroused as he nibbled on her neck. Maureen smiles at him, then tussled her hair.

"Hi, Joyce. I was just lying here in bed. What's up?"

"Well, I got this neighbor who isn't who he says he is. My curiosity got the better of me so I got access into his apartment." Maureen sat up in the bed the sheet fell down to her waist as Bruce nuzzled his face between her breasts. Maureen played with his hairy chest. Now it is Maureen's turn being aroused.

"So why are you calling me, Joyce? You should be calling the cops. I'm just an RN."

"Are you still seeing that smoking-hot detective – what's his name?"

"You mean Detective Bruce Pickett? Oh yeah, he's still in my life and I can't seem to get enough of him." Maureen grabbed his hand and placed it where it would give her the most pleasure.

"Well, if you see him, Maureen, will you tell him to call me back"

"I'll make it my top priority to give him a heads up."

"As they say, Maureen, a hard man is good to find." They both laughed at the corny joke then ended the call by hanging up.

When Bruce and Maureen are done getting laid, Bruce asked her about the phone call.

"That was Joyce, you know her, the firefighter."

"Oh yeah, the hottie with the sexy body," he said.

Maureen poked him in the ribs with a stiff elbow. "Keep it up and I'll cut you off from getting any of my TLC."

"Hey, I'm just kidding around. What did she want anyway?" He started to get dressed as Maureen entered Joyce's cell number into Bruce's lists of contacts on his phone.

"She really didn't say, so give her a call when you get a chance.

~ ~ ~

The detective logs in at his desk at the 61st Precinct. His partner walked into the squad room with a cup of coffee. "How are the kids, Chuck?" he calls. "I bet they're still upset after seeing all the carnage at the Garden."

"They asked me over and over, why daddy? Why are there bad people that want to cause us harm? What could I say to them, but reply I do not know the answer."

"Tell them that there are more good people than evil."

"Do we have any leads, Bruce?"

"It's too early to tell, but it appears to be the work of the same bomber who hit St. Pat's and Macy's."

"How about our cases, Chuck? Any new developments?"

"Nada, nothing, partner."

Captain Millwood stepped out of his office and pointed to them. They closed the office door behind them. "You were at the Garden when the bomb went off."

"Yes, Captain," Pickett replied.

"Did you see anything or anyone that might raise a red flag?"

"No, Captain. We were at the concession stand. My kids were in their seats when the bomb was detonated."

"Okay, that's what I wanted to know in case the brass at 1PP should ask."

They exited his office and Bruce placed a call to Joyce Owens. She answered the call while she was polishing the ladder truck. She described how she found the Santa suit along with a FedEx uniform, plus the airline stewardess uniform in Ari's bedroom closet. She also told him that Ari was wearing the Santa suit the day Macy's was bombed.

"Maybe it's just a coincidence," Bruce said.

Joyce replied, "Bruce, he doesn't receive any mail. He speaks with a foreign accent. I inquired about him at the maintenance office where I pay the rent. I found out that he is subletting the apartment from a corporation called Allied International."

" Now you've got my attention, Joyce."

"There is one other thing. Him and his so-called girlfriend on New Year's Eve were seen by me carrying two duffel bags."

"Thanks, Joyce. Are you at home?"

"Nope, I'm at the firehouse. It's my turn to do the tour, 3 days on, then 4 days off."

"Okay, take care of yourself, Joyce."

"Same here, Bruce. 10-4."

27

Dr. Hamilton advised Milton Stone that he will be confined to a wheelchair for the unforeseeable future. The bullet that is lodged in his lower back is less than 5 centimeters from the spine. He was released from the hospital. On the drive back home, Teddy told Sid, Fletcher, and his father how Finn McCoole and another man had attempted to kill Stone.

"Then it was McCoole who shot me. That makes perfect sense. He resented Morosco being taken out by us. Teddy, did they see you in the hospital?"

"No, Poppa. We moved you out of harm's way."

"We, Teddy? Who helped you?" Sid asked his brother.

"A Miss Belinda Bellows. She paid a visit but you were still heavily sedated, Poppa."

"Fletcher, you make sure that she receives a nice gift from me."

"Sure, boss. I know just the thing she likes," Fletcher replied as he looked at Stone in the rearview mirror.

They arrived at the home where Sylvia and Karen are waiting for them at the front door. Once they are settled, the men sit around the dining room table while Sylvia prepared the lunch.

"You know, Pop, that McCoole and his bunch will be gunning for you, so we need to get the drop on them before they do."

Milt asked Sylvia for one of his cigars and a glass of sherry. "I don't know about that, mixing liquor and all the medication you're on, Milt, will only send you back to the hospital."

"I guess you're right, Sylvia. Make me a cup of tea instead."

"How do you propose we should fix the problem, boss?" asked Fletcher.

"What if we reached out to McCoole? You know, tell him that you were shot and ask him if he might know who it could be," suggested Herb.

"I like that and I want to say thanks for calling the ambulance. If you weren't there I might have died."

Herb looked at Sid knowing full well that what the doctor said only reinforced that he wasn't in any way connected to the shooting.

"Okay, so everyone go about your normal routine. It's business as usual."

While they were having their lunch Sylvia observed a black Chevy Impala double-parked outside the house. Inside the car are Finn and Declan.

"How do you want to play this?" Declan asked Finn.

"Now is not the time to finish the job. Head on over to the Two Timer's."

Declan hit the gas and they drove off.

Karen is having contractions as the baby has moved into the birth canal. It won't be long before she will become a mother. Herb drove her to Coney Island Hospital where Maureen Flynn helped her into a wheelchair. Karen's doctor arrived and told her it shouldn't be long before the baby arrives. Herb is a nervous wreck as he paced the floor in the waiting room. God, let me get through this, he said to himself.

As Karen was being prepped for surgery, Maureen held her hand. "You know my father is a doctor," Karen said. "He is associated with the hospital."

"Oh really? Maybe I know him. What is his name?"

"Milton Stone," she answered.

Maureen recalled how he had tried to hit on her and gave her his phone number. "I know your father, but I haven't seen him in a while."

"Did you hear about the recent shooting up in Harlem?"

"No, I don't pay much attention to the news. I see more than enough violence right here in the ER."

"It was my father who was shot."

"Oh my God, is he going to be alright?"

"He was very lucky. The bullets did not hit any of the vital organs, but he has to use a wheelchair to get around."

"Did the cops get the shooter?"

"No, not yet."

Karen is moved into the OR. Within two hours she delivered a baby girl who weighed 7 pounds 6 ounces. Herb was overjoyed and could not wait to tell the family. But first he wanted to pay a visit to Finn McCoole. Herb is out to get Finn for shooting Stone.

Inside his car Herb unlocked the glove compartment and reached for the gun, then he drove down Kings Highway toward Finn's bar. So many thoughts popped into his head. What if I shoot McCoole and there are witnesses, then what? What if he pulls his gun and I get shot, then what? I know, I'll just play it safe and tell him I'm there for the doctor's take of the drug money. Yeah, that's the ticket. That way all things remain the same.

Herb entered the bar. Connor O'Roarke is filling the beer glasses from the taps for the regular barflies. "Hey, Connor, is Finn here?"

"Yeah, he's in the office."

Herb tucked the gun inside the back of his waistband and pulled his shirttail down to cover it. "Hey, Finn, how are you?"

Finn is seated in an old barber chair, busily counting a pile of money. Seated next to him is McDermit.

"Say, did you hear what happened to the doctor?" calls Herb.

"Yeah, that was something, him getting shot and all," replied McDermit.

"Who do you think did it?" Herb asked.

"Probably some wannabee uptown mugger trying to score by taking out an old white guy," commented Finn.

On the shelf behind the desk where McCoole was seated is Stone's black satchel. That caught Herb's eye. "Say, isn't that the doctor's medical bag?"

McCoole spun around in the barber chair to glance at it. "I guess it is, so what?"

"I was just thinking that when I dropped him off that night, he was carrying that bag. Now here it is on your shelf."

McDermit got up out of his chair, walked over to the door, and locked it.

Herb had no other choice but to pull out the gun. He had caught them red handed. "Don't make a move or you'll both get it. Now do as I say: fill up the bag with the cash."

McCoole looked at McDermit.

"I mean it. I got nothing to lose by taking you out, so be quick about it."

McCoole took the money and put it into the satchel, then handed it over to Herb. "You're a dead man, Herb. You and the other Kikes take notice. I know where you live with your mother, so you better watch your back because we'll be gunning for you and your wife and the Stones."

Herb told McDermit to step aside as he left the office. He then made a hasty getaway in his car.

"This is war from now on. Gravesend will be a fitting place to spill the blood of the Jews. I only regret that I didn't empty my gun into that son-of-a-bitch," McCoole said to McDermit.

28

Holly Fast paid a visit to the sheriff's office to surprise her husband Jasper. She had just made a pecan pie, his favorite dessert. Buford the bulldog is sitting at the foot of the sheriff's desk. He barked as she entered the office. Jasper is deep in thought. "A penny for your thoughts, dear," she said.

He looked up at her. Pushing himself away from the desk, he took the pie from her and placed it on the desk. "I just received word from a State Trooper I know that a car had been found out on Quarry Road on the outskirts of Echo Lake."

"Quarry Road ... isn't that where the old drive-in once was?"

"Yup where we used to go when we were dating remember?"

Holly's face turned red. "That's where we did it for the very first time. I knew right then and there you were the one for me." She gave Jasper a peck on his cheek.

"Well, the trooper didn't just find an unoccupied vehicle, Holly. There were two teenagers inside."

Holly had to sit down. "Oh sweet mother of God, do we know them?"

"Afraid so. It is Tammy Taft and Jeff Crawford, the same two kids who discovered the body up at Peekamoose Mountain Park."

"That's awful, Jasper. Do you have any idea how they might have died? Maybe it was from a motor vehicle accident."

"According to Brody Pence, the state trooper, it was drugs – probably fentanyl – that took their lives."

"So young and so sad, Jasper," Holly lamented.

"And so stupid. Holly, these kids today are using drugs like they're going out of style. You know Malachi Eaglefeather?"

"Yes, of course, dear."

"Well, he told me that the youths on the reservation are overdosing on an average of 5 a day. I tell you it is an epidemic that is plaguing the country. It is spreading like the wildfires out West. If we could only get our hands on the pushers who are dealing the deadly drugs then we could put a stop to it."

Holly sliced off a piece of pie for Jasper and then another for herself. Buford looked up at her with his sad eyes. "Oh, okay, you can have some as well."

Jasper poured two cups of coffee, set them down of the desk.

"How is that murder case coming, Jasper?"

"The one about Nick Morosco" he replied.

"Yes, that's the one."

"I went to the casino the other day at the request of Malachi. We talked to a suspect, a black man who denied he knew the victim. But we both knew that he was lying. I saw him with another white guy over at Lucy's diner. I figured right there that they were up to no damn good."

"Well, Jasper, you got your line in the water. It's just a matter of time before they bite and you can reel them in."

"But we had them, Holly, right then and there inside the casino, but I couldn't hold them. All I have so far is circumstantial evidence. There were no eyewitnesses when the murder was committed, just Malachi who can place the black guy and the deceased in a Mercedes Benz along with a third party who was involved."

"I see. Did you ever think about running the license plate of their car?"

"The Mercedes Benz, Holly?" he asked her.

"Yes, Jasper, that one," she replied.

"So you think that maybe the car was at the Turning Stone Casino when we questioned him?"

"Exactly, my dear. Don't you think that after watching all those reruns of Columbo plus Law and Order in bed that I couldn't piece together some overlooked evidence that a pretty sharp sheriff might have missed?"

Holly finished off her piece of the pecan pie. Jasper called Malachi and asked him if there was any video when the car was at the casino. He told Jasper that he will look into it and call him back.

Jasper was on his third cup of coffee when Malachi called him. "Hey, Jasper, the car is registered in New York – FYX372 MD."

"A doctor's car, how about that, Malachi? I'm much obliged. I'll see what the DMV website will tell us." The sheriff typed in the information on his computer, then waited for an answer. "I have it, Malachi. The car is registered to a Dr. Milton Stone on Surf Avenue in Brooklyn. I'll pass this on to the detectives at the 61st Precinct who are working on the Morosco case."

Then they end the phone call. Jasper looked at Buford and smiled. "In all the years I have known Holly, she never seems to amaze me. Gosh, if she could only cook." Buford barked in agreement.

~ ~ ~

The tip from Sheriff Fast leads the team of detectives to the door of the Stone's residence. Pickett rang the bell until Sylvia turned on the outside light. "Who's there?" she asked.

"The NYPD. We need to speak with Dr. Stone," Dobbs replied.

Sylvia looked at her husband, then said, "We did not call 911, so why are you here?"

"It's official business. We are investigating a homicide," Pickett told her.

"A homicide," she said.

Sid stood next to her at the front door. "How do we know you're cops?" he said.

The detectives pulled out their shields as proof, holding them to the glass windowpane on the front door. Sylvia unlocked and opened the door to let them in. "I'm Detective Dobbs; this is my partner, Detective Pickett. We'd like to speak with Dr. Stone. Is he here?"

"Yes, but my husband has just been released from the hospital and he is still weak. "

"Thank you, Mrs. Stone. This will only take a few minutes," Dobbs explained to her.

The doctor is in the living room with Teddy watching a television show. Sid followed the detectives, then sat down on the sofa. Stone turned the wheelchair around to face them.

"Dr. Stone, we are investigating the homicide of Nick Morosco. Did you know him?" asked Dobbs.

"No, I am not familiar with the name. What did he do?"

"He was an ex-con, a small time crook. Breaking and entering residences and businesses. His body was found upstate a few months ago," Pickett told him.

"I see. So where do I come in, detectives?"

"Your car had been spotted in the vicinity to where Mr. Morosco's body was found. And most recently your car was caught on video entering and exiting the Turning Stone Casino."

Before Stone had a chance to respond, Sid had something to say. "You come into my father's house and accuse him of murder? Why aren't you going after the guy who shot him instead of wasting precious time?"

"Where did this happen?" asked Dobbs.

"Up in Harlem, he was shot in the back just like Jesse James."

"Unfortunately the Bronx is out of our jurisdiction. Have you been notified by the Bronx detectives?" Pickett asked.

"No, not yet," replied Sid.

The front door opened and in stepped Herb. He had in his hand the doctor's satchel filled with cash. "Detectives, this is our son-in-law Herb," Sylvia informed them.

"Are you here to lock up Finn McCoole?" Herb asked them.

"No, who is he?" Dobbs asked Herb.

Herb walked over to the doctor and laid the bag in his lap. "I found this inside the Two Timer's. It was on a shelf in McCoole's office clear as day."

"Did you say the Two Timer's? Isn't that the bar on Kings Highway?" Pickett asked him.

"That's the one. McCoole shot my father-in-law in the back. He was carrying this bag the night he was shot. The only way McCoole could have obtained it is if he was the shooter."

"Okay, detectives, this is where it ends for now. If you intend to proceed with your investigation in regards to the car, you can contact my lawyer. I'll give you his number where he can be reached."

"That won't be necessary, Doctor Stone. We'll see ourselves out. Have a good evening," Dobbs replied and then they left.

29

A memorial to honor the victims who died and were injured by the recent bombings is scheduled to take place at the Freedom Tower in lower Manhattan. The president, governor, mayor, along with the police commissioner, are expected to attend. After extensive investigation conducted by the ATF, FBI, and the NYPD, it had been determined that the same terrorists committed all three of the bombings. The components were skillfully crafted by an exceptional mastermind.

There were so few clues left behind, other than the image of a suspect disguised as Santa Claus at the Macy's bombing and the pair of duffle bags left behind at MSG. When the latest information had been passed on, Detective Pickett's eyes lit up like a match in a coal mine. He remembered Joyce telling him about her neighbors toting duffle bags out of their apartment. Could it be mere coincidence or were they in fact the terrorists?

Pickett informed Dobbs, then Captain Millwood. With this latest development in the case of the three murders of Morosco, Dunham, and Fishman, the detectives have their work cut out for them. Millwood told them to concentrate on the murders at hand and to relay Joyce's tip to the Queens detectives.

Any good detective will tell you that time is crucial and a split second wasted only grants a suspect a window of opportunity to get away. Pickett called

Joyce, but she is unavailable so he doesn't leave her a message to call him back.

Shalimar has returned back to Ari's apartment after completing a trial run disguised as an airline stewardess. She took copious notes on her laptop in regards to how the air marshals are assigned seats on international flights. She related that to Ari as they prepared for another attack in Manhattan. Ari is especially interested in sending a message that will show not only the country but the entire world that a President of the U.S. could be taken out surrounded by an army of guards.

Ari's sister Ziva has closely been following the latest string of bombings and has come to believe that there is but one who could be responsible. Thus far no one has come forward to proclaim the acts, although ISIS has posted on their websites that a member is following their orders to kill as many of the infidels all in the name of Allah.

Ari and Shalimar shop online for lithium batteries and women's wigs. They will also purchase nails bolts and fertilizer from the local Home Depot. The tip from Joyce to Pickett is never passed on to the Queens detectives because Pickett and Dobbs have been told to bring in Finn McCoole for questioning in regards to Stone being shot up in Harlem. Inside the interrogating room, they begin the proceedings.

"Do you know Dr. Milton Stone?" Dobbs asked him.

McCoole is no dummy so he replied, "Say I do, will it incriminate me?"

To which Pickett said, "We have a witness who puts you up in Harlem at the scene of the crime. And we have the doctor's medical black bag that was in his possession the night in question."

"That's crazy. Okay, I know Stone. We do business every so often."

"What kind of business, McCoole?" Dobbs asked.

"I think I want a lawyer. I can see where this is headed."

"We didn't read you the Miranda Rights, so you're free to go. But you are forewarned it is just a matter of time until you are behind bars. Attempted murder is a serious crime," Pickett told him.

"How about murder, detectives? Suppose I was to tell you who killed someone? Would that surprise you?"

"Give us a name McCoole," Dobbs said to him.

"Will you drop the attempted murder charge against me? If not, then I'm walking out the door."

The two detectives stepped outside to confer. "What do you think, Bruce? Is he for real or just yanking our chains?"

"He has to tell us who was murdered and the name of the killer. Then we can take it to the DA. It will be up to him to make the call."

They stepped back into the room. "You tell us who was murdered and who the killer's name is. Then we will contact the DA. Deal or no deal, McCoole?" Pickett said to him.

"Nick Morosco was a friend of mine. I introduced him to Stone. Nick was the bag man."

"The bag man for what?" Dobbs asked him.

"I control a couple of bars and strip clubs. The doctor supplied pills to be sold. I made the deals and gave the money to Morosco, who then would turn it over to Stone. When some of the cash went missing, Stone accused Morosco. I told him no way; he wasn't like that. But Stone didn't believe me. So he took him out."

"And you were there when it went down?" Pickett asked him.

"Hell no," McCoole replied.

"Then how do you know that the doctor killed Morosco?" asked Pickett.

"He told it to me, in not so many words over lunch at Lundy's."

"Did he say where or when or how he did it?" asked Dobbs.

"No, he did not. He just said that Morosco had to go, so he took him out."

"You have to do better than that, McCoole. All we have is your word to go on. We have an eyewitness who will testify under oath that you were at the scene of the crime when Stone was shot," Pickett told him.

"Is it Herb Fishman that fingered me? That Jew bastard, he'd do anything for Stone. He took Morosco's place, picking up the dough. Did he tell you that, Detective? Did he tell you that his old man was murdered? My guess is that Stone took him out."

"Who is Herb Fishman's father?" Dobbs asked.

"Shelly Fishman. He had a kosher deli."

"That was the stiff who was found in the Caddy behind the Two Timer's?" Pickett replied.

"Now you got it, Detectives. Morosco and Fishman were taken out by Stone."

"Do you know a Mary Dunham?" asked Pickett.

"Mary was ... how can I put this? ... she was a regular at the bar."

"Did she know Stone?" asked Dobbs.

"I doubt it."

"How about Morosco, did she know him?" asked Dobbs.

"Yeah, she knew him."

"Were they intimate?" asked Pickett.

"How the hell should I know?"

"We're just trying to tie the three murders together," Dobbs told him.

"Look I'm telling you all that I know ... I'm telling you the truth. Hell, I'll even take a lie detector test to prove it."

They are about to wrap up the interrogation when McCoole has more to tell them. "You want to know who took out Albert Anastasia?" he said.

"Who the hell is he?" Pickett asked.

"You never heard of him? What the hell did they teach you in the academy? Google the name, go ahead. Anastasia was in the Italian mob. Joey Gallo and another hired gun took him out while he was getting a haircut. I have the barber chair that he was shot dead in."

"According to Google, that the murder was never solved, even though there were several eyewitnesses," Pickett told him.

"I know who the other hired gun is."

"Okay, who is it?" Dobbs asked.

"That is my get-out-of-jail card. Let's make a deal."

"Give us a name and we'll take it to the DA," Pickett replied.

"Fair enough. The other hired gun was Tyrone 'Trigger' O'Neil. He's in his late 80's, has dementia and Parkinson's."

"Where can we get in touch with him?" asked Dobbs.

"Well, that's where it gets a little dicey. The last time I heard of his whereabouts, he was living in Ireland."

"There is no immunity for him, so we can bring him back and put him on trial for the killing of a mobster," Pickett said.

"I never thought I'd be a rat and turn on a fellow Irishman," lamented McCoole.

30

On the outskirts of Chirp is one hellacious bar, aptly known as the Hornet's Nest. During the dark days of the Depression it was a speakeasy where you could drink bathtub gin, moonshine or white lightning. Now it is the headquarters of the notorious biker gang, the Bushwhackers. The leader of the gang is Lynyard Lucian, an Oneida Indian. He is big and muscular, has multiple tattoos, and a mean looking scar on his forehead. This is a permanent reminder of a fight he was in that ended badly when a pitcher of beer was smashed in his face. The dude that did this to the Indian never made it out of the bar. His remains were scattered in the woods shortly after he was stuffed inside a wood chipper.

The heroin that was shipped inside the Swiss chocolate that McCoole had picked up at the dock in Red Hook made its way up to Cody's Cycle Shop. Now it is being pushed by the Bushwhackers. Brody Pence is deep undercover as he pulled up outside the Hornet's Nest on his Harley hog. His boot heel pushed the kickstand down as he got off. Brody is dressed in a cut-off sweatshirt, torn jeans, biker boots, and a worn baseball cap. There are half a dozen bikes lined up in front of the Hornet's Nest. Brody took a deep breath, then entered the bar.

The bar is truly a rat hole, dingy and drab, the smell of marijuana wafting through the air. There is a dartboard that has the image of Jane Fonda when she visited North Vietnam. It is still a sore spot to the Vietnam Vets who fought against the Viet Cong. Fonda was a pawn in the Communists game to blame the United States for the war in Vietnam.

The jukebox is playing the Rolling Stones' "Honky Tonk Women." The barmaid is Paige Hayes, a large woman with purple dyed hair. She has a silver stud in her nose and tongue, and is dressed in a Vikings football jersey, sweatpants, and flip-flops. At the end of the bar is Lucian sipping on his Jack Daniels and Coke. A couple of the bikers are shooting pool as they check out Brody. The undercover trooper sits on a bar stool in front of Paige. She wiped down the bar and tossed a wooden coaster next to Brody.

"What'll it be?" she asked him.

"What have you got on tap?" he replied.

"We got Rolling Rock, Genesee, and Bud," she told him.

"I'll take a Bud," he said.

"Bud it is." She poured him a glass.

The Indian slid his stool just a tuck away from where Brody sat. "You know it takes a lot of balls for somebody we never seen before to set foot inside our bar."

Brody took a sip of his beer. "Hey, no offense, but I saw all the bikes outside, so I just had to come inside and see." He took another sip of the beer. "I really want to meet the owner of that maroon Indian Chief. That has to be one hell of a sweet ride."

"That would be me, stranger. I'm Lynyard Lucian. And you are, stranger?"

"Brody Pence. I have heard that if I want to get my hands on some quality drugs, then definitely check out the Hornet's Nest."

Lucian downed his drink and motioned to the barmaid for a refill. The bikers shooting pool stopped playing the game. They walked over to the bar, the wooden cue sticks in their hands anticipating a sign from the Indian to beat the crap out of Pence.

"How do we know you aren't a narc trying to make a buy from us?" Lucian asked him.

"C'mon, guys, me a cop? Get real," he replied. "Look, I work for my cousin Cody at his cycle shop in Echo Lake. Go ahead, check me out. He'll vouch for me."

Lucian pulled a bottle of pills from the pocket of his motorcycle vest. "What are you looking to score? I got oxy, bennies, you name it."

"How much per pill?" Brody asked.

"Five bucks," the Indian said.

"I'll take 50 of the oxy," said Brody, handing the Indian the cold hard cash in tens and twenties.

Brody popped one of the pills into his mouth to assure the Indian that he isn't the law. "That is one sweet tasting pill, just like a piece of chocolate."

"That's because it was shipped in Swiss chocolate from Europe. If you need another refill, you know where to go."

Pence downed the rest of the Bud, then left the bar and took off on his Harley. The barmaid washed the beer glass in the sink. "You surprised me Lucian, letting a stranger buy from you without first checking him out."

The Indian pulled out his Ray Bans and told her, "I'm just casting my bait in the water. If he is not who he says he is, well, then we'll just have to fire up the old wood chipper one more time, I reckon."

31

It is just a few minutes past three in the wee small
hours of the night when Joyce steered her VW down
Cloverdale Boulevard. Outside her apartment is a car
double-parked with the motor running. Ari and
Shalimar walked out of his apartment. He is wearing
the FedEx uniform; she is dressed head-to-foot in a
black garment. They got into the car, Ari behind the
wheel, Shalimar next to him. Joyce had to decide what
to do, whether to follow them or let it be. Her instincts
kicked in. Joyce thought that they are definitely up to
no good, so she decided to tail them.

At the corner of Cloverdale Boulevard and Union
Turnpike the traffic light was changing green to red.
The Buick that the terrorists are in had just taken the
onramp of the Grand Central Parkway. Joyce flew
through the intersection against the traffic light and
was just a few car-lengths behind them. The traffic is
light on the parkway so Joyce decided to allow extra
space between her car and theirs.

Joyce called 911 on her cellphone. The dispatcher
answered, "What is your emergency?"

Joyce replied, "I am a firefighter who is following a
pair of terrorists on the GCP (Grand Central Parkway)."

"How do you know they are terrorists?" the
dispatcher asked her.

"Look, we don't have a lot of time. The driver is a
male dressed as a FedEx worker, his passenger is a
female dressed all in black. You need to dispatch a cop

car ASAP. We just passed the Francis Lewis Boulevard exit."

The traffic began to slow down as cars entered the six-lane parkway. Ari maneuvered the Buick into the far right lane and proceeded to the LIE (Long Island Expressway). Joyce followed a few cars behind. "They are now headed westbound toward the city. I just passed the Citi Field exit."

"You say you are a firefighter. I need to know your name and where you are stationed." Joyce is clearly pissed.

Ari is on the LIE that took him to the Queens Midtown Tunnel. The car is not equipped with EZ Pass so he must pay cash. Joyce however has EZ Pass so she decided to breeze on through the tollgate. If she can overpass them and get into midtown Manhattan before they do, then maybe another terrorist attack can be stopped. At the corner of 37th and 1ST Avenue, Joyce spotted a cop car. She pulled over to get the officers attention. She told the cop all about them just as the Buick exited the tunnel. Ari is headed downtown on the FDR Drive.

"There, that's them. You need to call it in," she told the cop. The cop alerted the command dispatcher. "I have a credible report that needs immediate action. A dark brown Buick is driving south on the FDR. The occupants are believed to be terrorists. I repeat the occupants are alleged to be terrorists."

"10-4, Officer. I am dispatching all available mobile units," the command dispatcher said.

Ari exited the FDR at Houston Street. His intended target is to get as close to the Freedom Tower where the memorial is to take place honoring those that were killed and injured by the bombings. The trunk of the car is loaded with explosives. Ari has a remote control in his pocket that will activate the bomb. Shalimar is dressed in a black burka that covered a suicide vest of C4. In her hand is a kill switch.

As they got closer to Houston Street, a police barricade blocked their progress. A traffic cop directed them to drive to a specified spot. As Ari attempted to out maneuver the police, he is now surrounded by a contingent of the NYPD. He hit the brakes, threw the car into reverse, spinning the wheels, but he is pinned in by a SWAT armored truck. The officer in charge ordered them to exit the vehicle with their hands up. Ari looked at Shalimar there was nowhere to run.

"Don't shoot we are not armed," Ari told the cops. He exited the car as a group of tactical police forced him to his knees, then they slapped the cuffs on him and escorted him away.

Shalimar will not be taken into custody. As Ari was being escorted away, Shalimar shouted, "Allah Akbar" (God is Great). Then she placed her thumb on the kill switch that ignited the bomb. She was blown to high heaven and the car explosives left a crater in the street. Several of the cop car windows were shattered. The cops who were in closest vicinity to the explosions were seriously injured.

Ari Habbib is placed inside a squad car and is frisked. The remote control is taken and bagged for evidence. He is transported to the Tombs in lower Manhattan where he would be grilled by a crack team of investigators. They will come to find out that he and Shalimar are among the many sleeper cells in America who through the financing of Allied International have been carrying on clandestine operations.

Ziva Habbib, Ari's sister, had been notified of his capture and she asked to speak with him. They have not seen each other for years. Ari is dressed in an orange jumpsuit, his hands and ankles shackled. They sat facing one another. A three-inch thick bulletproof partition separated them. They used the telephone receivers to communicate.

"Why, Ari? Why have you done such horrible things? You are an Israeli, our father was Mossad, I am Mossad. How could you become an enemy that despises everything that we stand for?"

"I have no regrets. I have seen what Israel has done to the Arabs. You have bombed villages and killed civilians, many who are women and children. The Israelis say that they are the Chosen People, but will not allow Palestine to become a nation. It was okay for Israel to become a state after WWII, but for the Palestinians there is no place for them. You built a wall that encompasses the entire perimeter around Israel. You are surrounded by Arabs who will one day obliterate each and every one of you. Don't you see, Ziva, there is but one God and his name is Allah."

"You have lost not only your mind but your soul. You killed innocent people who weren't Jews. You killed Americans, Ari, who never took up arms against the Arabs. You have been radicalized and for that I hope they sentence you to death."

"I would gladly entertain that, Ziva. I will become a martyr to the cause. I will follow the brave Shalimar Saddiq into heaven where I will be treated like a king."

"You will follow her and ISIS and all the rest through the gates of hell where you rightfully belong."

The conversation has ended. Ari is escorted back into solitary confinement. Ziva will return to Israel and will work with Mossad to track down the operatives working for Allied International.

32

Had it not been for Joyce Owens being vigilant in pursuing the terrorists and then alerting the NYPD, it is anyone's guess how many lives could have been lost had the car bomb been activated at the Freedom Tower memorial service. The talking heads in government wasted no time taking the credit on news media outlets. Detective Bruce Pickett reached out to Joyce and thanked her for being brave enough to have done the right thing by following Ari and Shalimar, then alerting 911. She will be awarded a letter of commendation by the FDNY. It will be the first rung on the ladder to advancement.

Now Pickett and Dobbs can devote all of their attention to indicting those involved in the triple murders and the hit on Dr. Stone. Finn McCoole was not processed into the system, but nevertheless he is still considered the Number One suspect in regards to the Stone case.

Herb and Karen have named their baby girl Esther. True to his word, Stone purchased a house in Brighton Beach, a town that is near to Coney Island. Now that McCoole and Stone are bitter enemies, no matter where they venture the family is armed.

The trip to the Turning Stone Casino by Sid and Fletcher was all for naught. It would be far too risky trying to conduct business in uncharted territory. Therefore they would have to push the drugs in Brooklyn and up in Harlem.

Pickett and Dobbs picked up where they left off when McCoole was being questioned about the Stone hit. "Maybe the doctor had something to do with Shelly Fishman's murder," Pickett said.

"How about we pay a visit to his widow and listen to what she has to say," Dobbs replied. Brenda let them into her home where Karen and Herb are tending to Esther. Brenda took the detectives into the kitchen where she was in the middle of preparing a beef brisket.

"Mrs. Fishman, we want to offer our condolences for your loss. How are you doing?" Dobbs asked.

"It has been very hard on me," she replied. Brenda wiped her hands on the dishtowel, then closed the pocket door of the kitchen so that Herb and Karen cannot hear them.

"Were you contacted by the police after your husband was killed?" Pickett asked her.

"Yes, I was. But no one returned my calls when I requested if there was any progress in finding Shelly's killer."

"Did you husband have any enemies?" Dobbs asked her.

"Just one. Milton Stone, Detective. Herb and Karen were having a tough go in their marriage. He took it out on Karen. Sid, the eldest son, got even and beat the shit out of him. Herb shortly after went into a rage and exacted his revenge out on Karen. She was in really bad shape and had to be admitted to the hospital. Then he panicked and took off. Herb came here and we had words. He took whatever I had in my purse and the credit cards, then disappeared out the door."

Brenda offered them something to drink. They declined her kind offer. "Shortly after is when Shelly was killed inside the deli," she continued.

"Did anyone work with your husband at the deli?" asked Pickett.

"That would be Leo Keller."

"Where can we locate him?" asked Dobbs.

"He rents a studio apartment on Brighton and 3rd. Why do you want to know?"

"Maybe he was there when the killer or killers came for your husband. If so, then he could provide us crucial information to capture them," said Pickett.

They got the address for Keller but the landlady said he moved out right after Fishman was killed. He left no forwarding address. It was a dead end. As they drove back to the precinct, the detectives went over their notes.

"If what Mrs. Fishman told us about her son is true, than I can understand why Stone went off the reservation," said Dobbs.

"Did you see the daughter-in-law's face? Holy shit, I can only guess how many times she was hit by that scumbag of a husband," replied Pickett.

"So Herb lashed out at her and Sid evened the score. Then Herb took out his anger on her again, only this time he puts her in the hospital," countered Dobbs.

"Then when the family visits her in the hospital, the patriarch cannot bear to see his only daughter in so much pain," said Pickett. "The doctor is out for revenge. He can't locate the son-in-law, figured his old man knew where the low-life was hiding, and paid him a visit at the deli," Dobbs figured.

"Yeah, Chuck, only Fishman didn't have a clue or else he knew but wasn't going to give his only child over to the doctor. So he was killed by Stone," surmised Pickett.

"Yeah, but with no eyewitness and no evidence we can't bring him in for the crime," sighed Dobbs.

33

The autopsy report by the medical examiner determined that drugs were found in Tammy Taft and Jeff Crawford. They'd had no idea how lethal a small dose of fentanyl could be. Two teenagers so full of life now added to the list of ODs associated to the drug dealer.

Trooper Brody Pence has turned over the oxycodone pill purchase to his troop commander to be catalogued into evidence. Now he is encouraged to up the ante by purchasing additional samples of whatever Lucian has at his disposal. Lynyard Lucian told Brody that he will get back to him.

The ringleader of the Bushwhackers pulled up in front of Cody's Cycle Shop on his Indian Chief. Cody is busy working on a customer's Norton. The engine won't start and Cody has to figure out why. Cody's hands are covered with grease and oil.

Lucian entered the cycle shop and paused to check out the Dylan Triumph showcased in the center of the shop.

"Did you know that Henry Winkler, who played The Fonz on *Happy Days*, rode a Triumph," Cody said to Lucian.

"No, I didn't know that," he replied.

"And that same Triumph was used by Steve McQueen when he jumped over the barbwire fence in the film *The Great Escape*."

"No shit, Cody. How cool is that?"

"So what brings you here today?"

"I met your cousin Brody. He said you steered him to me so I sold him a couple of pills."

"Hey, that's great. I knew you wouldn't disappoint him."

"Yeah, and now he has placed an order for whatever I've got in stock."

"Hey, that's a good thing. Right?"

The Indian paced back and forth. "How well do you know him, Cody? I mean, I never saw him before. Heck, I know all the dudes who ride bikes up and down these back roads."

Cody wiped his hands on a dirty rag. "That's because he just moved here. He grew up in the City. We were never really close and all. Our dads were brothers but seldom got together."

"So what made him move up here into the boondocks?"

"Beats the shit out of me. The next time you see him ask him."

"You gave him a job, Cody?"

"Yeah, more or less, He comes in every once in a while. He's been picking up spare jobs here and there, cutting down trees, renovating homes, and what not."

"Well, he paid me in cash, no questions asked."

The Bushwhacker's cellphone rang. It is a text message from Finn McCoole, letting him know that he has a job for him in the City. Lucian then texted back, What does the job entail? McCoole replied that he needed an exterminator to get rid of a rat. Are you up for the task? The Indian texted him back, Sure no problem, just tell me when and where and how much you are willing to pay for my services. How about this weekend at Coney Island on the Boardwalk for 20 large? I'll be there Lucian replied.

~ ~ ~

At the Two Timer's, McCoole has decided that Herb Fishman needs to be killed. He knows that sooner or later the detectives will issue a warrant for his arrest for the attempted murder on Stone. If Herb is knocked off, naturally McCoole will be the prime suspect but he will make darn sure that he has a rock solid alibi to back him up. He needed to find someone who the cops don't know, someone who is cool under pressure, that is loyal to him.

Tootsie Snow, who has a brain for business and a body for sin, works on Wall Street at the brokerage firm of Meryl Lynch. Tootsie was almost indicted for insider trading when Ivan Bosky and Michael Milken were nabbed by the Feds. But the Feds couldn't find any corroborating evidence to implicate her. She has been raking in the dough, buying and selling stocks and bonds, plus pushing the dope for Finn on the side.

Finn and Tootsie meet up at Nathan's in Coney Island, he didn't let on to her about the Indian, Lynyard Lucian. Strolling along the boardwalk is Herb, Karen his wife and with their baby daughter Esther. McCoole had Lucian follow them as they take in the ocean view, walking among the beachgoers on the sand, enjoying a picture-perfect sunny Sunday afternoon. It has been a while since Herb and Karen were able to get some time by themselves to enjoy the Boardwalk. Now with a newborn, it only added to what had been lacking in their marriage: responsibility and trust.

At West 10th, there is Coney's Cone Homemade Ice Cream, Luna Park, the Wonder Wheel (Admission $7), Ruby's Bar and Grill, and The Clam Bar. The hot midday sun has Karen craving for ice cream so Herb obliges her suggestion. Karen told him she will change the baby's diaper inside the women's restroom on the Boardwalk. Herb will meet them outside after he purchases the ice cream treats.

While he is standing in line, the Indian poked the barrel of his gun into Herb's back. "No false moves or I'll pull the trigger now move" he told him. Lucian directed Herb away from the Boardwalk to where a van was parked. Inside are two members of the Bushwhackers. Herb was thrown into the back of the van and is roughed up by the bikers while the Indian drove them away.

Karen exited the women's restroom expecting to see Herb holding the ice cream. But he is nowhere to be found. She looked up and down the boardwalk. Where can he be? she wondered. She stood outside the men's restroom, thinking that he must be inside. But after a few minutes she is now worried. She called her father.

"Hello, Daddy. Do you know where Herb is? We were on the Boardwalk, me and Esther, when Herb went to buy us some ice cream. But now he is gone."

"No, Karen, I haven't heard from him." Stone doesn't like what he is hearing. Maybe McCoole has something to do with it. "Listen, Karen, why don't you just go home. Maybe Herb wasn't feeling good."

"Maybe you're right, Daddy. I'm sorry to have bothered you."

"You can never do that, my little girl. Call me when you get home. I love you."

"Me too, Daddy," she replied.

Inside the van Herb is pleading for his life. "What is going on here?" he said to them.

"Keep your mouth shut," one of the gang members said.

"Look, whoever you are, I got a wife and kid. If it's money you want, here take my wallet." He removed the wallet from his back pocket. He could kick himself for leaving his gun back home.

Lucian called McCoole to tell him that he has Herb. McCoole told the Indian to take him up to his place in the Catskills and that he will call him back later.

Then McCoole called Stone. "How you doing, Milt?" he said to him.

"Finn, you're calling me after trying to take me out. How dare you!"

"Look, let me get right to the point. I got your son-in-law. If you want to see him alive, I suggest that you listen to me real carefully."

"Go ahead, I'm listening."

"We both have a situation that needs to be taken care of. By now the cops are on to us dealing the dope around the City and Upstate. Your son-in-law can pin me for shooting you and I in turn can cut a deal with the DA to have you implicated in the murders of Fishman and Morosco."

"So what have you got in mind, Finn?"

"I'll give you Herb and you in turn give me the money he took from me at the Two Timer's. If not, there will be a turf war. I'll call in my troops from Sein Fein, the tough Irish lads I know back in Belfast."

"Don't think for a minute that I can't organize a bunch of Jews to take you on."

There was a lull in the conversation.

"We need to think this through and settle our differences with a sit-down in a neutral place, Milt."

"How about Nathan's?" he suggested to him.

""Nah, that won't work for me. How about Donovan's in Woodside?"

"No, that won't work for me either. We need a place that doesn't have a lot of customers, so we can conduct our business without being noticed."

Sid was listening in on the conversation. He recommended a local restaurant. "Finn, how about

Pepe's on Roosevelt Avenue, under the El in Jackson Heights?"

McCoole mulled it over. "That I can do, Milt. How about tomorrow night, around 9?" he said.

Sid told his father to make it later, sometime around 10.

"Okay, Milt. I'll see you there at 10. Don't forget to bring the cash and your satchel."

"What about Herb?"

"When I get the dough, you'll get him."

The conversation ended. Sid has a plan to take out McCoole. Teddy told them that he will do the job. "You Teddy? You must be joking. Have you ever held a gun?" Sid asked him.

"No," Teddy replied.

"So you are just going to walk up to Finn McCoole and blow his brains out?"

"Look, if Poppa goes into Pepe's, they have the advantage. No offense, Poppa, but you're in a wheelchair. If you go, Sid, they'll figure something is up for sure. But if I go in your place, they'll be relaxed and have their guard down most definitely."

"You know what, Teddy, my youngest son? I never thought I would see this day. You are becoming the man I hoped you would be."

Together with Fletcher, Sid showed Teddy how to handle a gun by gently squeezing the trigger. In the abandoned factory on Stillwell Avenue, they set up targets for Teddy to practice with. Eventually, he mastered the technique of handling the firearm. Now they had to find a way to get the gun into the restaurant before the sit-down.

Later that night just before closing time, Fletcher and Sid pull up in front of Pepe's. They placed an order to go. While Sid waited for the food, Fletcher entered the men's room. He lifted the lid off the toilet tank.

Then he placed the loaded gun and a pair of latex gloves wrapped inside a zip-lock plastic bag, then taped the package to the inside wall of the tank. He flushed the toilet to make sure the bag stayed secure to the tank. Then he slid the top back in place.

The next evening Sid, Fletcher, and Teddy arrived a little after 10. Teddy got out of the car. Pepe's is a small restaurant, a bar on the left, four tables, two on the right and two in the rear. On a Monday night it is usually dead and this night was no exception. McCoole is seated in the rear along with Declan McDermit. Teddy went straight to their table. They were surprised to see him.

"Well, what do we have here? If it isn't the Jew boy, and look, the curly fry sideburns are gone. What did you do, cut them off?"

"No, Finn, I have them tucked inside my baseball cap."

"I thought Jews could only wear yarmulkes," said Declan.

"Did you bring the money?"

Teddy placed his father's black satchel filled with the cash on the table. "What about Herb? My father said you would release him and let him go."

McCoole opened the satchel and counted the money. "It's all here. Let me make a call. A deal's a deal." He called the Indian who was holding Herb at the Hornet's Nest. "Okay, set the rat free."

"What about my 20 large, Finn? When do I get paid?"

"In due time, Lucian. I'll see you when I see you."

Teddy sat down at the table and listened for the sound of the trains that rumbled along the tracks of the El above Roosevelt Avenue. The waiter gave them the menus, which they looked over deciding what to have for a late dinner. Teddy's hands were full of sweat and his knees were shaking under the tablecloth.

"What's the matter with you, kid? You don't look so good," McCoole said.

"Yeah, I think I have to use the bathroom."

"First things first, frisk him," McCoole said to his partner in crime.

McDermit patted Teddy down. "He's not armed, Finn."

Teddy walked into the men's room and closed the wooden door of the stall. His stomach began to have butterflies as Teddy realized what he had to do. He held onto the stall, then puked all over the toilet. He wiped his face and shoes and the cuffs of his pants. Then he removed the lid from the toilet tank and pulled out the zip-lock plastic bag. He opened it, slipped on the latex gloves, and grabbed the loaded gun. The smell from the puke is nasty, so he went to the sink to wash his face. He dropped the zip-lock plastic bag into the trash bin. Then he waited until he heard the 7 train approaching the station on the El.

He took two deep breaths, then opened the door. McCoole and McDermit are busy eating their dinner as Teddy raised the Colt .45. McDermit's face was frozen in fear as Teddy pulled the trigger. The bullet entered just above his right ear. He slumped over his plate of seafood fra diablo. McCoole pushed his chair back to the wall, but there was nowhere for him to hide. Teddy took two steps forward.

"Mother of God, please don't do this. I'm begging you!"

"You shot my father in the back, Finn. You didn't have the guts to face him. But not me. I want to make sure that the last thing you see is my face."

Teddy pulled the trigger twice. The first bullet hit McCoole in the Adam's apple; the second hit him squarely in his forehead. McCoole was knocked off his chair. The white walls were splattered with his blood and brain matter.

Teddy picked up the satchel, and then dropped the gun on the table. The bartender and the waiter cowered behind the bar in fear of their lives. The cook in the kitchen hid in the pantry, silently saying a prayer. Teddy nonchalantly took a handful of the chocolate chip cannoli from the silver tray on the bar, then exited the restaurant.

A heavy rain began as Teddy hopped into the getaway car. Sid patted his little brother on his shoulder. "You did good, kid. Pop will be proud of what you done."

34

The 115th Precinct dispatched a team of female detective's to Pepe's. When they arrived, a uniformed patrolman was guarding the premises. Laverne Tatum is black, slender, and tall. Her hair is styled in a close-cropped Afro. Her partner is Desdemona Jones, a heavyset Caucasian with large facial features. Her hair is dyed bleach blonde.

"Were you the first to arrive on the scene" Tatum asked the cop.

"Yes, Detective," he replied.

"Make sure no one enters or exits until we have conducted our investigation," Jones said to him.

The three employees are inside the kitchen. They are still in shock and disbelief as to the double murders. There are drops of blood on the black and white marble tiled floor that lead from the door to the table. The detectives carefully step around the traces of evidence. They don latex gloves. Tatum picked up the gun and checked the clip. There are three bullets in it. And three shell casings lay on the floor next to the table.

Jones picked up McCoole's cellphone lying on the table in a pool of his blood. She pulled out a plastic bag, zipped it open, and placed the phone into it, then zipped it closed. The detectives checked the pockets of the dead Irishmen, removing their wallets to identify them.

"I got a Declan McDermit who resided in Woodside," said Tatum.

"I got a Finn McCoole who also lived in Woodside," Jones replied.

"From the looks of the shots fired, it was done at close proximity to the victims. There doesn't appear to be any stippling or GSR (gunshot residue) on either victim," said Jones.

Tatum entered the kitchen to talk with the staff, but they are reluctant to answer any questions. They are illegal aliens from Mexico. Tatum assured them, speaking in Spanish, that she doesn't care about that. "ICE will not be notified. Just tell me what you saw."

The waiter recalled the two men at the table who arrived about ten minutes before the third man. He was dressed in a dark jacket and pants, wearing a baseball cap and dark sunglasses. He had a black bag in his hand.

"Did you see a gun in his possession?" Tatum asked. The waiter replied he did not and that it all happened so fast. The detective thanked him.

Jones entered the men's room, where the strong smell of vomit made her gag. She looked around for any traces of evidence. She checked inside the wooden stall where the vomit was. Then she checked the trash bin where she found the plastic bag tossed by Teddy Stone. It is still wet. She made a mental note of it. Jones exited the men's room.

Tatum is crouched down next to McCoole's body. "Hey, Jones, check this out," she called, pointing to a red footprint. "We need to take a photo of this and send it off to forensics where maybe they can blow it up to capture what type of shoe the killer was wearing."

Jones showed her partner the wet plastic bag found in the trash.

"Let me see that" said Tatum. She un-zipped the bag, then placed the murder weapon inside. "It fits like a glove," she commented.

"So these two are seated at the table when the shooter comes in, but is or isn't carrying a piece," surmised Jones.

"The waiter told me that the killer was carrying a black bag. Maybe the gun was inside of it," Tatum pondered.

"If that is the case, how did he manage to get the jump on them? McDermit has a hole in the back of his head just above the right ear and McCoole over there took two slugs to the throat and dead-center above the bridge of his nose."

"What if the gun was planted somewhere that the deceased would never had suspected to look," suggested Tatum.

"Well, this plastic bag is wet, so maybe in the men's room," replied Jones.

The detectives retraced Teddy Stone's steps and pieced together how the gun was hidden inside the toilet tank. "Okay, so who the hell put it there for the killer?" asked Tatum.

"Maybe one of the help in the restaurant, what do you think?"

"What do we know about this place anyway? Maybe they were dealing drugs or running a whorehouse. Hey, we're talking about Jackson Heights, the melting pot of the City. Indians, Asians, Hispanics, soup to nuts, anything and anybody," Tatum conveyed her opinion.

"I think this was personal. Whoever did the hit knew these guys most definitely," stated Jones.

Tatum rifled through the wallets of the dead men. "It appears that the killer wasn't out to rob them ... cash and credit cards were left behind," said Tatum.

"We'll check the gun for ballistics and have the cellphones' history examined by the techs. Until then, let's take a trip to where they lived in Woodside," said Jones.

~ ~ ~

The detectives enter the vestibule of the apartment building and ring the doorbells to gain access. Through the buildings intercom they heard a woman's voice say to them, "Who is it?"

"The police," replied Tatum.

"I didn't call 911."

"Yes, ma'am. We are here investigating a crime that took place in the neighborhood. Can you let us in?" asked Jones. The inside door buzzed to let them in. The apartment on the right side of the lobby opened and standing there was Maureen Flynn. The detectives flashed their badges, so Maureen allowed them into her apartment.

"We are here in regards to your neighbors, McCoole and McDermit. How well do you know them?" Jones asked Maureen.

"Not much. Just hi when we see one another at the mailboxes. I'm an RN, so my schedule is kind of crazy, days off, nights on, just like your jobs."

Tatum was taking notes of what she had to say. "Anybody in the building that you might think could help us in finding out about them?" asked Jones.

"Not really ... maybe Tootsie Snow, but I don't think she is home. Her apartment is right across from them."

"Thanks for your help, here is our cards with our numbers in case you hear or see something," Jones said. And then they departed.

35

Lynyad Lucian was losing his patience, having just placed another call to McCoole that went straight to his voicemail. The Bushwhackers were egging him on to take Herb outside and fire up the wood chipper. Brody Pence entered the Hornet's Nest. Herb was seated in a chair, his wrists duct-taped behind his back. There are black and blue bruises to his face and his lip is cut.

Brody walked over to Lucian at the bar and asked him, What's up with that dude? Did he fail the initiation test to join the Bushwhackers?"

"Yeah, in a roundabout way, but enough about him. I got the pills you asked for. Are you ready to buy?"

Herb had to find a way for Brody to help him get out of his precarious situation. "I bet those drugs came straight out of Brooklyn. My father-in-law can really hook you up with as much as you want."

"Brody walked over to Herb. "No shit? What's his name?"

One of the Bushwhackers punched Herb in the stomach to shut him up. Brody shoved him into the pool table. Then a couple of the gang members went after the trooper.

A shotgun is fired into the ceiling by the bartender. "I've seen just enough of this in my place. Now either you settle up your differences like men or else take it outside."

Brody pulled out the cash to pay for the drugs, but he also wanted to have Herb set free. "How do you know about the drugs?" Brody asked Herb.

"I work for Dr. Stone. Him and Finn McCoole are in business together."

Brody looked at Lucian. "So what gives? Why is he here?"

"Look, this is none of your concern. Take the dope and blow."

The trooper isn't going anywhere. "Have you got the doctor's number? Maybe I can call him and clear the jam you're in."

The Bushwhackers were getting antsy. They are just waiting for Lucian to give them the word to take him out.

"That's what I've been trying to tell these guys. They got the wrong man."

Brody motioned to Lucian that he wanted to talk to him outside. "Keep an eye on him," the Indian told his gang.

"So what's with that dude?"

"He is a witness to a hit so, McCoole told me to pick him up and put him on ice for a while."

"Did you call McCoole back?"

"I did, but got nowhere."

"So you're going to continue to babysit that guy?"

"Maybe. What's it to you? You got what you came for, so get on your Harley and move on."

Lucian walked back into the bar. Brody realized that he doesn't have a lot of time. He drove out of sight and then he got in touch with his troop commander. But he received some bad news he is unable to provide him with extra men. It is beyond his control. The troop commander told Brody not to go in alone. Brody reached out to Sheriff Jasper Fast and brought him up to speed. The sheriff contacted Malachi Eaglefeather to pitch in.

Together, they concocted a plan to get the Bushwhackers out into the open instead of going into the bar with guns blazing. Malachi led the charge in his pickup, followed by the sheriff in his marked car, then Brody on his Harley. The Bushwhackers had their motorcycles parked in a row outside the Hornet's Nest. Malachi steered the pickup straight into the motorcycles knocking them over like bowling pins. The crunch of metal-upon-metal caused the Bushwhackers to exit the bar like a Chinese fire drill.

They were full of rage, ready to take on Malachi. He taunted them as he revved the engine. "Let's get him!" one of the Bushwhackers shouted. Malachi backed up, then peeled out, leaving a slick of black tire marks in the gravel. The Bushwhackers pry the twisted handlebars of the motorcycles apart, then start up the engines and took off, leaving only Lucian inside the Hornet's Nest. Malachi will take the Bushwhackers pursuing him through the twisting, turning backroads until they lose sight of him.

Meanwhile, the sheriff and the trooper get the drop on Lucian and bring him into custody. Herb is relieved that his ordeal is finally over. Lucian could not believe that Brody is a state trooper.

With backup from the K Troop State Troopers, the rest of the Bushwhackers were apprehended when they returned to the Hornet's Nest.

36

The Bushwhackers were charged with the kidnapping of Herb Fishman. Lynyard Lucian wanted to make a deal to shorten his sentence behind bars. He will flip the supplier of the drugs if the DA will agree to his demands. Brody Pence was shocked to find out that his cousin Cody was the middleman in the transaction of the drugs being shipped from Brooklyn to Upstate. Brody made sure he was the trooper who slapped the cuffs on Cody.

Now in custody, Cody wants to cut a deal with the DA. Cody's testimony allowed the investigation to enable the authorities to uncover the connection of Finn McCoole and Dr. Milton Stone.

The murder weapon used in the double homicide in the restaurant was examined. The serial number had been filed down, so there was no way to determine who owned the firearm.

As for the bloody footprint, it was a size 9 Hush Puppy. There were no security cameras inside Pepe's and the illegal Mexicans remained silent, refusing to help the detectives capture the triggerman. But McCoole's cellphone produced the connection to Stone. Queens detectives Tatum and Jones paid a visit to Dr. Stone. They basically asked him the same questions that Pickett and Dobbs had a few weeks ago. Only this time the names of Cody Pence and the leader of the Bushwhackers Lynyard Lucian were added to the list.

"Detectives, you are accusing me of taking out McCoole and McDermit? You tell me how is that possible? I am confined to this goddamn wheelchair, for Christ sake!"

"We have the calls that McCoole made to you," Jones told him.

"Yes, he called me to say he was holding my son-in-law for ransom."

"And why was that, Doctor?" asked Tatum.

Sylvia propped up the pillow in the wheelchair for her husband. "McCoole tried to take me out up in Harlem. Herb was an eyewitness, so McCoole figured if he offs Herb then the cops don't have a case against him."

The detectives had no more questions to ask Stone and then departed.

"Poppa, what should we do? They are building a case against you," said Teddy.

"They haven't got enough evidence to convict me. If they did, I'd be sitting in an eight-foot cell cooling my heels."

"You're damn right, Pop. There's no way they can jam you up on the murders. If they could find a way, it would already have happened," said Sid.

Sylvia has heard enough of this. "My God, what has happened to our family? First, it was dealing in drugs, then you get shot, and now you are talking about murder? Not one, but four murders. We are not the Mafia pretending to be a nice Italian family. We are Jews, not low life guineas." She shut the door to the master bedroom and tuned the lock.

~ ~ ~

The DA in Brooklyn has compiled enough evidence to indict Dr. Stone. So the doctor is taken into custody by Pickett and Dobbs.

The presiding judge placed a bail of $500,000 that was swiftly paid by Stone's attorney. A Harvard grad, Slocum Carrier is the high-profile attorney-at-law who defended rap star KY Jelly, beating a murder rap against his rival Hott Dogg.

Carrier assured Dr. Stone that the DA has a weak case and after the facts are heard inside the courtroom the jury will return with a decision to acquit him of all charges. The DA is Butler Church, a Fordham and John Jay grad, who was involved in the conviction of Bernie Madoff. He would love to add another notch of a high-profile case to his achievements by having Stone convicted to a life sentence.

So the stage was set for a trial in Brooklyn's King County Criminal Court of Appeals, located at 120 Schermerhorn Street. The presiding judge is the honorable Topanga Ramsey. She has been on the bench for thirty years. She has presided in the case of Leona Helmsley, the Queen of Mean, and also Martha Stewart. It was her decision to hand down prison sentences to those very successful businesswomen. Topanga has no compunction with any of her rulings and she anticipated that the case against Stone will be cut-and-dry, no matter what the outcome of the court proceedings proves.

The jury selection process was slow and tedious. The prosecutor and the defense were adamant as to who would serve in the trial. But after two weeks of deliberations the jury was set, eight men, four women, and an alternate. Seated in the courtroom are detectives Pickett Dobbs Tatum and Jones. They will be called to testify.

The DA addressed the court with his opening comments. "Ladies and gentlemen, Your Honor, members of the jury, the State of New York has been the target of three bombings by radical terrorists. Now, you are probably wondering, what has that got to do with this case? Well, I will take you step-by-step how in fact Dr. Milton Stone acted with depraved indifference as he spread drugs at random throughout the City and Upstate. Every one of the overdoses that took a life was because of him. He prescribed amphetamines and fentanyl. The victims weren't just junkies looking for a quick fix in an alley or an abandoned building or in the park. Oh no, the buyers were mothers, fathers, kids who were being treated for pain due to an injury. Once they started to take the pills to numb their pains, they were hooked. Then after the medical coverage was exhausted, they sought out the pushers. And guess who was their supplier? None other than Dr. Milton Stone. He had the means, the motive, and he carried it out to the letter. So as the money was being raked in, Nick Morosco was hired by Finn McCoole to pick up the receipts from bars and strip clubs that McCoole oversaw. My theory is that Morosco was skimming and that Stone caught on to his shenanigans. So the doctor took care of business. Morosco had to go. It was simple as that. But guess what, there wasn't a single eyewitnesses. Ditto to Mary Dunham, Shelly Fishman, Declan McDermit, and Finn McCoole. Five murders all attributed to the defendant seated in a wheelchair. Do not let his handicap fool you for a minute. He is a shrewd, calculating, cold blooded murderer who needs to be sentenced to life without a glimmer of parole."

Now it is the defense attorney's turn to address the courtroom. "The DA has not a shred of evidence against my client. There are no witnesses that can place Dr. Stone at the scenes where these murders took place. So I ask you members of the jury as we proceed during the trial to pay attention to the facts and ask yourself is the prosecutor attempting to sentence an innocent man? At the end of the day, my client will be confined to a wheelchair while the killer or killers are out there free to continue pursuing their wanton ways of life."

The prosecutor called the first witness to testify under oath: Malachi Eaglefeather. "Mr. Eaglefeather, would you tell the court when you first encountered the defendant," said Church.

"It was on October 19th around 7 p.m. A dark Mercedes Benz was idling in front of the Turning Stone Casino. I approached the car and saw three men inside."

"Can you describe them?"

"The driver was black and bald, There were two passengers in the back seat; one of them was scrawny and scruffy looking."

"How about the other passenger, Mr. Eaglefeather?" commented Church.

"I could not make him out because the windows were darkly tinted and he was seated in the shadows."

"Was that the only time you saw these men?"

"No, sir. About a month ago, the black man and another man were at the casino playing craps."

"So why were you concerned about that?"

"Well, you see that man in the back of the Benz on the night in question turned out to be Nick Morosco. The black man was captured on the casino's security cameras shortly after Morosco's death. He was driving a Cadillac Escalade that had been rented by Morosco."

"Thank you, Mr. Eaglefeather. I have no more questions for this witness, Your Honor."

"Mr. Carrier, you may proceed to question the witness."

"Thank you, Your Honor. Mr. Eaglefeather, my oh my, that is a rather unusual surname is it not?"

"To some it might sound a bit strange. I am an Oneida Indian. My ancestors have been on this land for many centuries."

"Yes, isn't that just dandy. Now could you tell us if the black man you saw is seated in the courtroom?"

Malachi scanned the occupied seats. "No, he is not present."

"Very good. How about the gentleman that was seated in the back seat of the car with Nick Morosco? Is he anywhere in the courtroom?"

"No, he is not. Like I said, I couldn't see his face."

"Very well. And how about the man who was with the black man at the casino, is he in the courtroom?"

Malachi pointed to Sid Stone. "There he is, seated in the front row behind the defense table."

"I have no more questions for this witness."

"You may step down. Mr. Church, proceed to call your next witness."

"Thank you, Your Honor. I call Jasper Fast to the stand."

The sheriff is sworn in. "State for the record your name, sir."

"I am Jasper Fast, sheriff for Chirp."

"Thank you sheriff. Now could you tell the court exactly what happened on the night of October 19th?"

Jasper had to refer to the little black memo book he uses to jot down pertinent information in regards to his job of sheriff. "Well now, it wasn't the 19th, but on the 20th. I got a call to check out a body that was found at Peekamoose Park."

"I see. And when you arrived at the scene, Sheriff, what did you find?"

"I found the body of a man who had his hands and legs tied together. He had a deep wound around his neck and he was missing a tongue."

A gasp could be heard in the courtroom. "Go on, Sheriff. Please continue."

"Well, there were no footprints near the body and there was no wallet or money in the pockets of the deceased. It wasn't until Malachi dropped by at the Sheriff's Office and we put the pieces together that it was Nick Morosco who was killed in my neck of the woods."

"Thank you, Sheriff. I have no further questions."

"Mr. Carrier, you may proceed."

"Thank you, Your Honor. Sheriff, have you ever seen my client in your town?"

"No, sir. If I did, I would have remembered him."

"I see. How about his son?"

"Now him I have seen along with the black man."

"And where was that, Sheriff?"

"The first time I laid eyes on them was at Lucy's Truck Stop Diner. They were in a dark Mercedes Benz. The next time was at the Turning Stone Casino."

"I see. And what brought you there?"

"Malachi is the head of security for the casino. I had credible evidence that the two men were involved with the murder of Nick Morosco."

"And what was that. Sheriff?"

"Well, we ... I mean, Malachi had the video of the black man at the casino driving the Cadillac Escalade and that he was using Morosco's credit card."

"Did you question him, Sheriff?"

"I did, but Sid Stone got agitated and told me that I had no jurisdiction in the casino because it is on Oneida property."

"So then what did you do?"

Jasper had to refer to his notes. "I was in contact with the NYPD detectives in Brooklyn who found Morosco's Caddy at another murder scene."

"Don't tell me the black man was driving it."

"Oh, no, sir. You'll have to ask the detectives who the driver was."

"Do you have anything to say, Sheriff, that might lead us to believe that my client was in any way connected to Morosco's murder?"

Again Jasper checked his black book for information. "That would be when Malachi and Trooper Brody Pence apprehended the biker gang – the Bushwhackers – who were holding Herb Fishman as a hostage at the Hornet's Nest. That was the first time I heard mention of Dr. Stone."

"Thank you, Sheriff. I have no further questions."

"You may step down, Sheriff. Councilor, you may call your next witness," said the judge.

Lynyard Lucian took the stand. He was wearing an orange jumpsuit with bold black letters saying OCC Orange County Correctional embossed on the back.

"State for the record your name."

"Lynyard Lucian."

"And you are currently incarcerated for what crime?"

"That would be for selling drugs."

"Who was your supplier?"

"That would be Cody Pence, who was the middleman who received the drugs from Finn McCoole."

"I see. So let me get this straight. According to Sheriff Fast, you were nabbed while holding Herb Fishman hostage."

"Yes, sir. I had a deal with McCoole to grab Fishman and take him out."

"And how were you going to dispose of him?"

Lucian realized that by stating what he had done in the past could lead to a stiffer penalty for murder. "I'd rather not answer on the grounds that I would incriminate myself."

"Your Honor, he needs to answer the question."

"Overruled. The witness does not have to answer. Proceed, Councilor."

"Why did McCoole want you to take out Fishman?"

"Because Fishman was there when McCoole shot Stone. If the Jew disappeared, then McCoole would be off the hook for attempted murder."

"So McCoole and Stone were in business together?"

"Absolutely. Where do you think the drugs came from?"

"Thank you, Mr. Lucian. I have no further questions."

Now it is the defense attorney's turn to grill the witness. "Lynyard Lucian, let me take a wild guess and state this isn't the first time you have been outfitted in an orange jumpsuit."

"That would be correct."

"And isn't it a fact that you cut a deal with the DA to accuse my client in order to serve a lesser prison sentence."

"Your Honor, I object," said the prosecutor.

"Overruled. Answer the question," said the judge.

"Yeah, I cut a deal, but the doctor was the guy who gave us the drugs to sell."

"Did you ever meet Dr. Stone?"

"No, I did not."

"So how do you know for sure that this is the doctor McCoole was doing business with?"

Lucian chuckled at the statement. "Because he's the guy who got shot by McCoole. Is it not obvious? Who else could it be, but Stone?"

You could hear laughter in the courtroom in regards to his remarks. "No more questions, Your Honor."

"You may step down," said the judge.

The prosecutor called detectives Pickett and Dobbs to the stand. They stated how they interviewed the doctor at his home. The defense had no questions for them. The faster they could move along the case, the better the outcome for Stone.

Next up were detectives Tatum and Jones. They described in detail the bloody scene at the restaurant. "Now, Detective Tatum, the cellphone that belonged to Finn McCoole contained calls made and received by the defendant?"

"Yes, that is why we went to interview Dr. Stone."

"And did he deny knowing Mr. McCoole?"

"No, he did not."

"No further questions."

"Councilor, your witness," said the judge.

"Thank you, Your Honor. Detective Tatum, let's cut to the chase, shall we? There is no way in hell my client killed McCoole and McDermit or any collusion thereof. All you have is a cellphone, no smoking gun, no fingerprints whatsoever to place Dr. Stone in the restaurant that night."

"Yes, but ..."

"No further questions."

"You may step down, Detective. Call your next witness," said the judge.

Detective Jones took the stand. "Now, Detective Jones, could you tell the court what else you found on the night in question?"

"We found a .45 Colt on the table and a plastic zip lock bag, still wet. We speculated they were planted inside the toilet tank in the men's room."

"I see ... so the shooter or someone had to have been there before the victims were shot."

"That is correct. We tried to interview the staff, but they are here in the country illegally and were fearful of ICE deporting them back to Mexico."

"I see. Was there any other evidence left at the restaurant by the killer?"

"Yes, a bloody shoeprint, size 9 of a Hush Puppy shoe."

"Thank you, Detective. I have no more questions."

Slocum Carrier buttoned his suit jacket. "Now, Detective Jones, if I were the prosecutor I would have asked you the obvious question that is dangling over our heads."

"And what would that be, sir?"

"What size shoe does the defendant wear? Venture to take a guess, Detective, tell me what do you think?"

"I really can't say from where I am seated."

Carrier walked over to Stone, who was seated in the wheelchair, and slipped off his shoe. He then handed it to the detective. "Could you please read aloud what is inside the shoe, Detective Jones?"

"Size 10 D."

"Thank you, Detective, for debunking the prosecutor's theory that my client is a murderer. After all, Johnny Cochran got OJ Simpson off by trying on a black glove on live TV. If it doesn't fit, you must acquit. No further questions."

Now it is the defense's turn to call witnesses to testify on behalf of Milton Stone. "Your Honor, I would like to call at this time Governor Mickey Como."

All eyes turned to the rear of the courtroom as the doors opened. The governor took the stand.

"I thank you, Governor Como, for taking the time to testify on behalf of my client."

"No problem," he replied.

"Governor Como, could you tell the court how you and Dr. Stone met."

"Me and Milt go way back. We grew up in the same neighborhood. We played stickball and pickup games of basketball in the schoolyard."

"Would you categorize in your assertion that Milton Stone showed any sense of depravity as a child."

"No, never. He was just a normal kid. Nothing stood out that I would consider a red flag."

"Thank you, Governor. No further questions," said Carrier.

Now it was the prosecutor's turn. "Governor Como – boy, I have to say I'd never thought I would be asking you questions in a murder and drug trial, but here we are. There is credible evidence to indict Dr. Stone. Is there anything that you would perceive to be illegal that could persuade you to think differently about your relationship with the accused?"

"I have been the Governor of New York for several years, as all of you know, and have commuted very few death-row sentences in return for a lifetime behind bars. I do not want to sway the jury in their decision by being a witness for the defense. I can only say that Milton Stone has been a good friend of mine. I feel for his family and his wife Sylvia."

"Did you and Dr. Stone socialize?"

"On occasion. From time to time, we have dinner."

"And the last time you saw Dr. Stone was when?"

"That was at the wedding of his daughter at the Catskills Country Club back in October."

"I see, Governor. Do you remember what time it was?"

"Let's see probably around 7 p.m." "

"October 19th to be exact, Governor, Which just so happens to be the same day that Nick Morosco was killed."

"All I know is that only a coward would shoot an unarmed man in the back. Finn McCoole got what was coming to him. It saved the taxpayers a lot of time having him tried, convicted, and sentenced to a life in prison."

"Thank you, Governor. You may step down."

The next witness called was Belinda Bellows. All eyes were fixated on her as she took her time walking to the stand. She was wearing a clinging torch-red dress cut low, exposing her ample breasts. The diamonds on her ears and fingers sparkled. She crossed her long slender legs, then tapped her long fingernails on the wooden railing of the stand.

"For the record, state your name."

"Belinda Bellows, but most of my friends know me as Sweet Magnolia."

The men in the courtroom laugh. Judge Ramsey tapped her gavel in a sign of authority.

"Now, Miss Bellows, how did you and the defendant meet?"

"Oh, me and Miltie go way back. He saved my life. If it wasn't for him. I'd be just another ho found dead up in Harlem."

"How so, Miss Bellows?" asked Carrier.

"I'd been hookin' ever since I got my period. My pimp hustled me here and there. When I was 15, my pimp beat the crap out of me, then pushed me out of his car in the middle of the night on the Cross Bronx Expressway. There I was half-naked, dodging cars, when all of a sudden there he was."

"There who was?"

"My angel. God sent me an angel in Dr. Stone. He covered me with his coat, put me into his car, found a place for me to stay, even gave me a couple of bucks for something to eat. I was down and almost out, but here I am to testify for my savior, Dr. Milton Stone."

The prosecutor now has his turn. "Miss Bellows, did you have sexual relations with Dr. Stone?"

"I have. And let me tell you the doctor has a bedside manner you would not believe." She glanced at Sylvia whose face had turned a scarlet-red, filled with rage and contempt. "A man married or single has urges. And he if doesn't get it at home, well then he can always order out … if you know what I mean."

The courtroom burst out in laughter as Judge Ramsey pounded her gavel to reclaim order.

"I have no further questions for the witness."

Miss Bellows stepped down as everyone followed her every move while exiting the courtroom. The defense attorney conferred with his client whether or not to put him on the stand to testify in his own behalf. The doctor had no reservations and told the attorney to proceed.

"Your Honor, I would like to call Dr. Stone at this time."

"Go ahead, Councilor," replied the judge.

Stone pushed his wheelchair in front of the judge's bench, then turned it around to face the courtroom. "For the record, please state your name."

"I am Doctor Milton Stone."

"Now, Doctor Stone, the District Attorney has portrayed you as a drug dealer and a murderer. How do you feel about these accusations?"

"I am a husband father and recently a grandfather. I have a small office in Brooklyn where I treat all types of illnesses. My patients are blacks, whites, Latinos, Asians, Indians, you name it. I turn none away."

"Now, Dr. Stone, what can you tell us about Finn McCoole?"

"Mr. McCoole came to my office complaining of back pains. He said he injured it at work. So I advised him about claiming it as worker's compensation. That way he would get paid if he didn't show up for work."

"And did he agree to that?"

"Yes he did. I wrote him a prescription for painkillers and he went on his way. I never thought much about it until the next day. I was missing one of my prescription pads on my desk. McCoole must have taken it when I left the room to look in on another patient."

"So McCoole stole the pad. Dr. Stone, did you report it to the police?"

"No, I did not. Now looking back, I should have. Maybe I would not be where I am today."

"Tell us about Nick Morosco."

"When Morosco first came to my office he was pacing back and forth in the waiting room. I knew right away he had a drug habit. He told me he was friends with Finn McCoole and that McCoole said I would help him out."

"And did you?"

"I told him point blank I am not a pill dispensary and to take his drug habit elsewhere."

"And did he?"

"No, he threatened me, said that the Irish mob would come for me and my family if I didn't do what he said."

"And you cooperated with him?"

"What choice did I have? I was concerned for the welfare of my family."

"So you were coerced to fill bogus prescriptions for Morosco and McCoole?"

"Exactly. McCoole would sell the pills in the bars and strip clubs throughout the city."

"Do you have any idea who may have killed Nick Morosco?"

"It had to be the Irishman, Finn McCoole. I think that maybe Morosco was skimming some of the money from the sales of the pills. McCoole got wind of it and decided he had to go."

"So why then was Morosco's body dumped upstate in the Catskills?"

"Beats me. Maybe he did it right before or shortly thereafter when he attended my daughter's wedding."

"I see. Where did the wedding take place?"

"At the Catskills Country Club. The Governor was there. He even mentioned it when he was on the stand, testifying on my behalf."

"How about Mary Dunham? Did you murder her?"

"I never met the woman. Who is she?"

"She knew Morosco and was a regular at the Two Timer's."

"That's one of McCoole's hangouts."

"Miss Dunham was murdered, brutally stabbed to death, and you have no idea why?"

"Like I said, I never met her. Maybe McCoole did it because she knew he killed Morosco."

"That seems plausible. Eliminate a witness who could testify against him. That leads up to Shelly Fishman. How well did you know him?"

"Shelly owned a kosher deli. He was a big gambler, bet heavy on the ponies and sporting events. His son Herb married our daughter Karen. He beat the crap out of her. My eldest son Sid got even though and did a number on Herb. But Herb got his revenge and put my daughter in the hospital."

"I see ... by you telling the court what transpired between your son and Shelly's son, his death could have been done by you for revenge."

"I had nothing to do with that. Shelly was up to his eyeballs in debt. When he was at the wedding, he told me how much money he was losing that day because the deli was closed. Ask his wife Brenda. She'll tell you how the business had to be sold to pay off his creditors. I gave Herb a job when no one else would."

"Now we come to the night when you were shot, Dr. Stone. Could you walk us through exactly how that happened?"

"I took a trip up to Harlem to see Miss Bellows, a dear friend of mine. Herb drove me. When I exited his car I started to climb the brownstone steps. It takes me a little longer because I have polio. Anyway, I remember it had started to rain. Then I heard two shots and felt a hot intense pain in my back. I lost my balance and dropped my bag as I collapsed. I faintly remember hearing Herb and then Miss Bellows, but I was losing consciousness. When I awoke, I was in the hospital."

"Do you have any idea who would want to kill you?"

"None. I have no enemies. But Herb figured it out. He went to the Two Timer's and found my black bag in McCoole's office, so I knew he had to be the triggerman."

"How about the night that McCoole and McDermit were gunned down. Were you involved in their deaths?"

"Do I look like I could kill someone? I am in a wheelchair. How could I have possibly pulled the trigger?"

"McCoole called you that night, Dr. Stone. What was all that about?"

"He told me he'd kidnapped Herb and that he would kill him if I didn't give him $20,000."

"Why did he kidnap him?"

"Herb knew that McCoole was the person who shot me that night."

"So why not just take Herb out? After all McCoole had nothing to lose."

"I think you would have to ask the Irishman. Only he knew how nuts he was. Did you know that he once was a terrorist back in Belfast? He was some crazy Mick along with his gang of thugs."

"Thank you, Dr. Stone. I have no more questions."

"Mr. Church, you are permitted to question, Dr. Stone" said the judge.

"Dr. Stone, what a tale you can tell. Extortion by the Irish mob, bodies piling up in Brooklyn, Upstate, and in Queens. There is blood spilled all around you ... and yet you sit there in a wheelchair and expect the court to have pity on you. Well, I see through your oh-so-clever charade of lies. You were never threatened. No, you were the master planner who recruited McCoole and Morosco to do your bidding. You even had Miss Bellows to peddle your poison. Isn't it a fact, Doctor, that on the night you were shot in Harlem your black bag was filled with drugs that would be sold to junkies out of her whorehouse? Isn't it also a fact that you were in the company of Nick Morosco when he was killed the night of your daughter's wedding?"

"No, I was not."

"We have an eyewitness, Malachi Eaglefeather, who testified under oath that Nick Morosco was in a vehicle driven by a bald black man. Do you not have a black man working for you?"

"Yes I do. Morgan Fletcher is his name."

The DA scanned the courtroom. "So he was driving your car that night when Mr. Eaglefeather encountered him?"

"No he was not. Fletcher was with me at the wedding."

"Are you implying that the eyewitness is lying?"

"What I am saying is that he was mistaken. How many times are black men depicted as the culprits to a crime only to be found innocent after the fact?"

Detective Tatum gestured to the DA. "Could I have a moment, Your Honor?"

"Make it quick, Councilor."

Tatum passed a folded piece of paper to the DA. He opened it to read what she had written. The only proof to connect the doctor to the murders is his car. The DA folded the paper, then slipped it into his pocket. "Your Honor, may I approach the bench?"

The DA and the defense stand at the sidebar in front of the judge. "Your Honor, if we could inspect the defendant's vehicle for traces of blood from the victims, then we could put the case to bed."

"Your Honor, this is highly irregular. The prosecutor has a paper-thin case against my client and now at the conclusion of the trial he wants to add into evidence the vehicle?"

"I understand your concern, but under the circumstances, I will allow it."

Slocum Carrier related to Stone the judge's decision. The doctor was clearly upset.

"Mr. Church, have you anything else to ask this witness?"

"No, Your Honor," he replied.

"Dr. Stone, you may return to your seat at the defense table."

The doctor's vehicle was impounded in the courthouse parking garage where the NYPD had cordoned it off to be inspected, searching for traces of blood and DNA. Luminol was used, a chemical that has the ability to uncover any stains that might not have been detected with the naked eye.

After more than several hours the NYPD had come up empty. The court was notified of their search of the vehicle. Now it is up to the jury to decide the doctor's fate.

37

After three days of deliberation the jury was still deadlocked. Judge Topanga Ramsey had a full caseload on her calendar, so she sent the jury back for a final time to come up with a solution. It was fruitless. They could not agree on the counts of dealing drugs and the multiple murders. The judge had no other choice but to declare a mistrial. Milton Stone lowered his head in relief as Sid and Teddy shouted for joy.

At the curb outside the courthouse, Fletcher waited for them. Sid and Teddy assisted their father in the wheelchair. Slocum Carrier and Butler Church are standing by.

"I had him by the short hairs, damn it, but he got away. I know that son-of-a-bitch is guilty … I just know it. But I have to hand it to him. He played us like Charlie Daniels uses his fiddle. Who knew that he'd trade in the Mercedes Benz for a blue BMW just before the trial was to begin?"

"Do you intend to prosecute him again, Butler?"

"The jury is still out. You never can tell, Slocum."

Milt told Herb to ride back home with Fletcher and Sid. He would ride in Karen's minivan with Sylvia, Teddy, and baby Esther. "There is more room in the minivan for the wheelchair, so you three take the BMW."

As Fletcher drove away, Herb was seated in the front passenger seat next to him. "That was a great idea your father had, trading in the Benz for the BMW,"

Fletcher said. "Those Keystone Kops made a huge mistake by asking to search the wrong vehicle."

Herb handed a package to Sid in the backseat. Sid unwrapped it. Inside was a cigar box containing Cubans: Cohibas Montecristo and Punch. This was a gift from the dealership for being one of their best customers. Each of them made a selection.

"I have to hand it to Slocum Carrier as to how he proved to the court that Pop wears a size 10d shoe," said Sid.

"Yes, and he kept me far away from the courtroom so that I could not be called to testify," commented Fletcher.

"No hard feelings, Sid?" asked Herb.

"After what you did to my sister I really wanted to take you out, Herb. But you stepped up big time by saving my Pop's life and proving that Finn McCoole was the shooter."

"Thanks, Sid. That means a hell of a lot to me."

Sid pulled a fancy gold lighter out of his pocket. "Wow, where did you get that?" asked Herb.

"It belongs to the DA, Butler Church. I noticed that whenever a witness was testifying he would flip the top of the S.T. Dupont Linge gold lighter with his thumb. That is his *tell*."

"His *tell*, Sid? What's that?"

"A *tell* is what gives you away, that something is bothering you and you react with a subtle gesture that you might not realize," explained Fletcher.

Sid flips open the lid of the lighter, watching the tiny flame dance. He lit his cigar, then Herb's and Fletcher's.

"It doesn't get any better than this," said Herb.

"Now that the trial is over, what will your father do?" asked Fletcher.

Sid took a moment as he enjoyed the ride. "Knowing my Pop, he'll keep on doing what he does best, making a fast buck no matter what."

Herbie said, "He's been so good to me, Sid. He could have refused to pay the ransom to McCoole after all I put him through. If you know what I mean."

"I do, Herb, but like he said you were there for him. Anyway let's forget about the past and let bygones be bygones." Herb and Sid bump fists in a gesture of solidarity.

Fletcher steered the import onto the Belt Parkway. The traffic slowed to a crawl. Off in the distance they could see billowing black clouds of smoke. A fire at the Coney Island Hospital was intensifying, out of control. By now it had become a five alarm. The siren sounded inside Engine 279 Ladder 131. Captain Dante directed the firefighters to man their trucks. Joyce Owens only had seconds to fetch her helmet, boots, and turnout coat, then hop on the back of the fire truck.

Detectives Pickett and Dobbs were alerted that a Brinks truck had just been hijacked by a team of armed bandits. They took off in hot pursuit.

A traffic cop directed Stone's BMW to exit the Belt Parkway. As they proceeded north on Ocean Parkway, the light at the intersection of Avenue Z turned from red to green. At the same time the Happy Hooker fire trucks are heading east and the stolen Brinks truck is heading west. The BMW was T-boned and then pancaked – the roof pushed up, the windshield crushed and shattered. The fuel tank was ruptured, causing gasoline to seep into the backseat. The lit cigars ignited the volatile liquid, transforming the BMW into an deadly inferno.

The firefighters scrambled to extinguish the flames. The Jaws of Life tool was used to cut through the steel frame of the car. The armored truck bandits were apprehended by Dobbs and Pickett, then placed in the backseat of a squad car.

Joyce spotted Bruce next to the smoldering car. The fire at the hospital was being brought under control. Bruce's cellphone received a text message from Maureen Flynn letting him know that she is all right. Joyce wiped the sweat from the lining of her helmet. "They never had a chance," she said to Bruce.

The firefighters removed the charred bodies from the still-smoldering BMW. It is then that the detectives realized who the occupants of the car were.

"A perfect storm comes to end three lives lived on the edge," observed Dobbs.

"They almost pulled it off, Chuck. If not for the chance encounter of a fire truck and the armored truck, who knows what other lives would have been lost at their hands?"

The fire in the hospital was deliberately set by a disgruntled former employee who wanted to get even.

Governor Como and Mayor Burattino commended the firefighters who risked their lives saving the patients and the staff by fighting the fire. "If not for our finest, many lives would have been lost. But also there was an unfortunate tragedy that could have been prevented had the NYPD and the FDNY followed departmental procedures. Three innocent men – two brothers-in-law and a friend – were killed in a horrific traffic accident that involved members of the fire and police departments. I am ordering an investigation into this matter. I am recommending those who were involved be suspended immediately," said the Mayor.

Well, that was all Sylvia and Brenda needed to hear. They immediately got in touch with the high-profile attorney Gloria Allred, who drew up legal papers to sue the City of New York for wrongful death of their sons Herb and Sid.

And they say that crime does not pay.

CONCLUSION

After the funeral and sitting in Shiva for Sid Stone, the family in their time of grief picked up the shattered pieces and attempted to move on with their lives. Sylvia was going to play a game of Mahjong at Rochelle's.

"Why don't you bring Karen and Esther with you, Sylvia," suggested Milt.

"Who will be here to take care of you?"

"I'll be fine. Teddy is in his room so the three of you should go. Have a good time."

Sylvia was reluctant, then decided to go with her daughter and granddaughter. "Maybe Brenda might like to get together with us at Rochelle's. I should give her a call. She must be a wreck, all by herself now that Shelly and Herb are gone."

Sylvia, Karen, and the baby leave the house as Milt watches them through the living room window.

"Poppa, is there anything you need?"

"I'm getting tired. Help me get into bed."

Teddy moved the wheelchair over to the motorized chairlift at the foot of the staircase. Then he helped his father out of the wheelchair and into the seat. At the top of the stairs was another wheelchair that Teddy used to get Milt into the master bedroom. Teddy helped his father out of his clothes and into his pajamas.

"You are a good son, Teddy. Why don't you go out instead of staying home with me?"

"That's okay, Poppa. I don't mind."

"Why don't you take my car and pay a visit to Belinda Bellows. I'm sure she would be delighted to see you."

"Oh Poppa, I couldn't do that."

"Sure you can, but don't go empty handed. Go fetch my black bag." Teddy did what Milt told him to do. "Teddy, on the top shelf in the closet, there are bottles of pills. Grab a handful and put them into the bag."

Teddy did just that for his father. "Are you sure I should be doing this?"

"Teddy, I want you to be prepared to provide for the family. One day you will be the last man standing. Sid is gone and Karen doesn't have a son to carry on our name, so it will be left up to you."

"I should pay Dr. Hamilton a visit at Bronx Lebanon. She was instrumental in saving your life, Poppa."

"That she was, son. Stop off and buy, her some flowers at the hospital gift shop and tell her thanks."

"So you'll be all right if I go, Poppa?"

"I'll be fine, but before you go, do me a favor."

"Sure, just name it."

"Go into the liquor cabinet and bring me the decanter of brandy, a glass, and a cigar from the humidor."

Teddy made sure his father had everything he needed before he left.

Milton had settled in his king-size bed. Turning on the flat-screen high-definition LED television with the remote, he clicked through the channels until he saw the breaking news on one of the cable channels. The newscaster was relating the latest events.

"The New York bomber Ari Habbib who had been incarcerated at the maximum security prison GITMO in Cuba has escaped. There are conflicting reports as to how he managed to pass through undetected while the prisoners were being escorted back into their cells. Obviously, Habbib had help. President Trump had sent off a Twitter that Ari Habbib is a very bad dude and he believes that Allied International provided the means.

Trump also added on Twitter that George Soros is a major player in the network of terrorists. You could also thank the Clinton Foundation for this breach of trust by colluding with the known enemies of America. And finally, a Cold Case Murder more than a half-century old may finally be solved. The notorious gangster Albert Anastasia was gunned down at a New York hotel's barbershop while getting his hair cut in 1957. There were two assassins who shot him, but they were never captured. Joey Gallo bragged that he was one of the shooters and eventually was killed in a hail of bullets in Little Italy. Now the other fugitive of the law has been captured. In a tiny cottage in Roscommon, Ireland, Tyrone 'Trigger' O'Neil was living undetected. When the authorities arrived to take him away he replied, 'What took you so long to find me?' O'Neil proudly displayed the nickel-plated pearl-handle .45 Colt that was presented to him by the Luciano and Costello Mafia families."

Milton turned off the television, poured himself a brandy, then lit the cigar and tried to relax. But the bullet lodged close to his spine was causing him pain. So he took some oxycodone along with the fentanyl and washed it down with the brandy. It only took a few minutes for the drugs and the booze to take effect. In his dreams were the visions of ghosts that visit him. Nick Morosco was the first to appear. His neck had the deep ligature mark where the piano wire choked him to death. His mouth was wide open, missing the tongue that was cut out.

"Why are you here?" Milt uttered. But the ghost of Morosco could not answer him. "You deserved what you got for stealing from me!"

Then the ghost disappeared and in its place Mary Dunham came through. "Who are you?" asked Stone.

"I am Mary Dunham. Because of you, I was murdered by Finn McCoole and Declan McDermit. They took turns stabbing me until I died."

"I am not to blame. I don't know you. Be gone from me!"

The ghost departed only to be exchanged by the ghost of Shelly Fishman. The face was missing; it was grotesque. The doctor tried to look away but could not. "Shelly, why didn't you tell me where I could find your son? You would still be alive today if you had. You have no one to blame but yourself for what happened." The ghost of Shelly Fishman faded.

Then a pair of ghosts came into view. It was the two young teenagers Tammy Taft and Jeff Crawford.

"Who are you? I have never seen you before."

"We are the victims who, thanks to you, overdosed after taking the drugs you supplied," said the ghost of Jeff.

"I had no idea. The drugs were supposed to go to the junkies and the losers who had nothing to live for."

"We are not the only ones, Dr. Milton Stone. There are many more who have overdosed thanks to you," said the ghost of Tammy.

Then they faded away and in their place stood Finn McCoole and Declan McDermit. Their wounds from the bullets of the gun that Teddy used are visible.

"I have neither qualms nor regrets as to what my son did to you," Stone said. "You deserved what you got for killing Mary Dunham. How could you?"

"How could we not?" McCoole replied.

"We made a deal, but you broke it by killing Morosco," said McDermit.

"Be gone with you now. Satan's calling you from the depths of hell."

"We'll be waiting for you, Stone, to join us there. It'll be like old times again," said McCoole.

The last of the ghosts to visit Stone was that of Fletcher, Herb, and Sid. Their clothes are ripped to shreds. The ghosts are nothing more than smoldering embers.

"Fletcher, my dearest friend, can you ever forgive me?"

"What is there to forgive you for, boss? I knew what I was getting into when I agreed to work for you. This is where I belong. I'll take my lumps for what I did when I walked among the living."

"Herb, I am so sorry for what happened to your father. If he would only have told me where you were, then he'd still be alive."

"So it was you who killed him?"

"I had no other choice, Herb. You would have done the same thing if someone were to harm your daughter Esther."

"He didn't deserve to die in such an agonizing way, Milt."

"I know, Herb. Can you ever forgive me?"

The ghost of Herb turns away, refusing to face him. They were on fire and in a lot of agony.

Stone was deeply upset as he called out to his eldest son. "Sid, my boy, I am so sorry for all that I've put you through. Can you ever forgive me?"

Sid raised his arms, trying to reach his father. "Pop, you still have time. Repent and change your evil ways before it's too late. There are so many who are stuck in this place, so many who will forever endlessly roam because of how they wasted their lives."

"Sid, my son, I am so sorry. I should have never let you enter into the business of dealing drugs. You would still be alive, same with you, Fletcher, and you too, Herb."

The image of the ghosts slowly began to fade.

Stone flailed his arms and in so doing knocked the lit cigar out of the ashtray and onto the carpet. The ashes of the cigar began to smolder and spread to the edge of the bed quilt. It was now aflame as the fire expanded. The sedatives were taking effect on Stone as he tossed and turned in and out of consciousness.

Then he lay still, immobile in the bed. "Am I hallucinating or is my bed on fire?"

The flames licked at the pillowcases as the bedroom transformed into Stone's personal crematory. Gone are the cherished possessions, the photographs of Sylvia and Milton on their wedding day. Gone are the photographs of Teddy Karen and Sid when they were first born. Gone are the three pairs of bronze baby shoes and the letters written by Sylvia and Milton's parents that described in detail the horrors they endured in the concentration camps. All of it gone, consumed in the inferno that was stoked for years by Milton Stone.

Ashes to ashes, and dust to dust.

Thank you for reading.
Please review this book. Reviews help others find
Absolutely Amazing eBooks and inspire us to keep
providing these marvelous tales.

If you would like to be put on our email list to receive
updates on new releases, contests, and promotions,
please go to AbsolutelyAmazingEbooks.com and sign
up.

About the Author

James R. Fox received an Associate Liberal Arts degree from Queens Borough Community College. Now retired, he devotes his attention to writing, music, photography, traveling, and reading. Among his publications are *The Wake*, *Wisdom of Wishes*, *Christmas Eve*, and *The Map of the Carpenter*. His "Key West" was selected for inclusion in *The 2013 Robert Frost International Poetry and Haiku Contest* anthology.

ABSOLUTELY AMAZING eBOOKS

AbsolutelyAmazingEbooks.com
or AA-eBooks.com